my name is ROSE

Also by Sally Grindley

my name is ROSE

Sally Grindley

BLOOMSBURY

LONDON BERLIN NEW YORK SYDNEY

Bloomsbury Publishing, London, Berlin, New York and Sydney

First published in Great Britain in June 2011 by Bloomsbury Publishing Plc
36 Soho Square, London, W1D 3QY

A CIP catalogue record for this book is available from the British Library

ISBN 978 1 4088 1402 4

Typeset by Hewer Text UK Ltd, Edinburgh
Printed in Great Britain by Clays Ltd, St Ives plc, Bungay, Suffolk

1 3 5 7 9 10 8 6 4 2

www.bloomsbury.com
www.sallygrindley.co.uk

For Angela & Michael

Chapter 1

Rose nestled her head sleepily against her mother Esme's shoulder. The accordion on Esme's lap had fallen silent, but a whisper of song escaped her lips still. On the bench opposite them, Rani, Rose's younger brother, was fast asleep, buried deep in a riot of red and yellow cushions. Their father Nicu's silhouette, solid and comforting, filled the open front of the wagon. He was quiet, contemplative, eyes fixed on the winding road ahead, a shadow of the man who, five hours earlier, had brought crowds to their feet with his lusty ballads. A plume of tobacco smoke wafted from his pipe and trailed into the back of the wagon. Rose caught a whiff of its musky aroma and breathed it in. She loved that smell, especially now as it mingled with the familiar sweet and sour of Esme's home-made perfume.

They had had such fun! From the moment they had

arrived, the village streets welcomed them with festoons of multicoloured flags strung haphazardly from tree to lamp post to balcony. Villagers waved from doorways and children ran up to hold the horses' reins, skipping alongside them, chattering excitedly. The procession of wagons was herded into a small meadow dotted with wild flowers, a handful of which Rose had collected and presented to her mother. In the village square, a pig was being roasted over hot coals. Rose, Rani and their cousins and friends watched its skin blister and hiss, and wondered how long it would be before they could sink their teeth into its succulent flesh. Close by, a large metal pan filled with popcorn rattled so hard it threatened to explode. There were rows of tables piled high with fruit and vegetables, bread and cakes, sweet-meats and candied fruits, and others that were quickly loaded up with copper and clay pots, rugs and throws, bangles and beads, which the Roma had made and brought with them to sell.

On another side of the square, away from the hubbub, Rose had watched her Aunt Mirela lay out her tarot cards under a garish makeshift awning, ready to tell people their fortunes. In the corner was a crystal ball, which her aunt rarely used but which spoke of mystery and enchantment. Rose loved to stare deep into it and imagine another world there, one filled with fairies and other mythical creatures, a world where everything was magical. She loved feeling the cool, smooth roundness of the ball, and hoped that one day she would be able to tell people what life had in store for them just by gazing into it, though she sometimes puzzled over why they would want to know. That day, queues stood patiently outside Aunt Mirela's tent from the moment she had set herself up till dusk settled over them and the day came to a close.

Meanwhile, families quickly started to gather in the two cafés that bordered the third side of the square, turning their chairs outwards to face a long wooden stage that had been erected by the statue in the centre. In the bars, village men chased their coffee down with shots of something stronger and waited expectantly for the entertainment to begin. The clink of glasses, the clatter of plates, the babble of voices, the roars of laughter all grew louder as preparations were completed. When at last Nicu, Esme and other members of their clan leapt on to the stage, the crowd erupted with shouts and cheers. From the youngest, toothless babe in arms to the oldest, toothless man in a wheelchair, everyone took part in the annual carnival and dance.

And how they had danced! The square became a sea

3

of bodies rising and falling, leaping and whirling. Rose had been swung round in circles so many times that one of her cousins had to help her to a chair until the world stopped spinning. From there she gazed at Esme's fingers fidgeting endlessly over the ivory keys of the accordion. Her mother moved seamlessly from jigs to reels to haunting ballads, taking her cue from her husband, he too capable of changing the mood in an instant. When Nicu passed the singing to another member of the band, he picked up his violin and played with people's heart-strings, stretching notes until they quivered and sighed, before changing the tempo, sawing vigorously with his bow and stamping out an accompaniment with his feet.

Rose was so proud of Esme and Nicu. She watched them whip the crowd into a frenzy, then stroke them into tranquillity. She watched the smiles on every face and the joy in every smile. They were like sorcerers, her mother and father, weaving spells with their music that made the world a happy place. *I want to have that power one day*, she thought. She wanted to have that power even more than she wanted to follow in Aunt Mirela's footsteps. She would make people laugh and love. She had been learning to play her father's violin since she was five, and she had more talent in her little finger, he said, than he had in all of his fingers and toes put together. In that instant, she made up her mind that when Nicu next offered to teach her, instead of resisting and ignoring his look of disappointment, she would embrace him and ask to continue with her journey right there and then.

Chapter 2

The eerie hoot of an owl came first and wavered over the idle *clip-clop* of the horse's hooves. It wasn't connected. Or was it? A warning, perhaps? Rose had scarcely had time to register it before the startlingly bright lights careered round the corner. A prolonged screech of rubber on tarmac, a cry of alarm, a frantic hauling on reins was followed by the hideous smash of metal into wood. The air shuddered briefly, before giving way to a calamitous silence.

And then, had she been able to hear and understand, Rose might have heard the words 'Wretched Gypsies!' spat, not spoken, from too close by. Had she been able to see, she would have known that a man and a woman, he in a dinner suit, she in a long silk dress and dainty high heels, were sitting in their car, checking themselves over for injury and staring at the wreckage around them.

A loud tremor of breath from somewhere outside the car window made them tremble in turn, before the night fell silent again.

'What was that?' the woman sobbed. 'It wasn't the horse, was it?'

'Never mind the horse,' hissed the man. 'I think my leg's broken.'

'You were going too fast.' The woman began to sob hysterically. 'I told you not to go so fast.'

'They were in the middle of the road. It wouldn't have mattered what speed I was doing.'

'You were going too fast,' the woman insisted. She grabbed the door handle and tried to open it.

'What do you think you're doing, Daphne?' The man put his arm across to stop her.

'I'm going to see if they're all right,' she cried. 'Why can't we see anyone moving?'

'You're not getting out,' the man ordered. 'They might be dangerous.'

'They might be dead,' the woman wailed.

'In which case there's nothing to be done.'

Chapter 3

Rose tried to block out the blinding light above her. It made her anxious and she wished Esme would switch it off. Even from under the curiously stiff, white sheet the light still struck her with its harshness. She listened to the strange sounds that filtered through her crudely fashioned shroud. Someone, somewhere, was wailing. A bucket clattered and a voice chastised. Not Esme's voice. A phone rang. *Where's the phone come from? We haven't got a phone. Papa doesn't like them.* 'They stop you from being free,' he said. 'They take away your choice to be left alone.'

Rose suddenly noticed that one of her arms was bandaged. And then, when she shifted, she saw there was blood all over the sheet on which she was lying. She screamed when she saw the blood. She screamed and the phone rang and voices cried and a horse whimpered and the wagon rose high in the air and she was flying and spinning and falling, falling, and the trees glowered and there was pain and silence.

She couldn't move now. Someone was pinning her down. She could smell sour breath on her face. She began to struggle, kicking with her feet, flailing with her arms, until the pain became unbearable and she lay back exhausted.

'That's better,' she heard. 'We can't help you if you fight us.'

Rose tried to focus. A large, grey-haired woman was leaning over her, pressing down on her chest with her hands. The woman relaxed, wiped her hands on the apron she was wearing, and stood up straight when she was confident that Rose had calmed down.

'Who are you?' Rose whispered.

'I'm Sister Orta. And what's your name?'

Rose bit her lip. She didn't want to tell this stranger.

'You've had an accident and you're in hospital,' Sister Orta continued. 'If you tell us your name, we can find someone to look after you.'

Rose frowned. 'My mother and father will look after me,' she said.

For a moment Sister Orta shifted uneasily. Then she took a deep breath and said, 'I'm afraid . . . I'm afraid your mother and father are dead. The boy – your

9

brother – too.' She didn't give Rose time to react before she added, 'The police are waiting to speak to you.'

Rose attempted to get out of bed. 'Why are you telling me this?' she sobbed, grappling to free herself from the sheet. 'Where's Mama? I want my mother.'

'Now don't start getting yourself into a state,' Sister Orta said patiently. 'You've lost a lot of blood and you need to keep still. Besides, there are other patients to think about.'

Rose no longer heard Sister Orta's words. Her one thought was to find her mother and father, to get away from this woman with her sour breath. Esme's face drifted before her and she reached out to grasp her.

'Mama!' she cried.

But then she felt something sharp bite into her arm. She yelped and fell back heavily on to the bed.

'You'll feel better after some sleep.'

Rose stared helplessly as Esme drifted away and disappeared down a long, dark tunnel, followed by Nicu and Rani. She wanted to call after them, but no sound came, and then there was nothing.

When Rose woke again, she found the same stark white light, the same stiff white sheets, the same disjointed sounds. The nightmare hadn't ended. She turned her head to one side, hoping to find Esme sitting close by, watching over her. There was another bed, its occupant facing away from her.

'Mama?' Rose allowed a whisper to escape, before she realised that this person had straight, mousy-brown hair. Esme's hair was thick and black and wild. Esme's hair tumbled down her back when she freed it from its beaded clasp. Her mother complained about the rogue white strands that she discovered from time to time, and laughingly blamed her children for causing them, but Rose had never noticed them.

'Are you feeling better now?'

Rose looked the other way. A woman was sitting in a chair by the bed. She had a large plaster across her forehead and another on the back of her hand, which was clutching a white handkerchief. She had been crying, Rose thought, because her eyes were red and puffy. She was pale too, her thin face framed by unnaturally yellow blonde curls. She was dressed in a severe navy suit, the sort Rose had seen when they rode the wagon through towns once in a while.

'You've been asleep for a very long time. I was worried about you,' she said.

Rose frowned. Why should this woman – a gadje she

11

had never met before – be worried about her? Gadje people didn't concern themselves with Romani folk. The woman spoke the language of their country fluently, yet with a strange accent.

'Who are you?' Rose asked.

'I'm a friend,' the woman replied. 'A friend who wants to help you.'

Rose saw tears welling up in her eyes and wondered why she was upset, but she didn't want to share her sadness, whatever it was.

'I want Mama,' she said simply. 'Where is she? And Papa and Rani?'

Rose looked beyond the strange woman to where a large, grey-haired woman was issuing orders to a young nurse. She recognised Sister Orta, who turned, saw that she was awake and came striding over.

'Are you ready to tell us who you are now?' Sister Orta asked.

'Where are my parents?'

Sister Orta stared at her. The strange woman shifted uncomfortably in her chair.

'I told you,' the nurse said firmly. 'They died. In the accident. You're the lucky one. You escaped.'

Chapter 4

Rose didn't speak after that. She couldn't. There was nothing to say. Words no longer seemed to have any meaning; not those spoken by the strangers who came to her bedside once in a while, nor those that scrambled themselves together in her head or fled to far corners of her brain and refused to reassemble.

She lay in her bed and stared at the ceiling, at the cold, white light that stripped the world of colour. It made little difference when it was switched off at night. Rose could still feel the shadows flitting between the beds, checking for life and death. She could hear the hushed voices, the hum of monitors, the shuffling of papers. Occasionally, a harsh cough or a sharp cry penetrated the barriers she had built around herself and threatened to haul her back to reality, but mostly she resisted their assault. She preferred to keep her eyes open, even when it was dark, because when she closed them, her mind seized the moment to catapult her through a tunnel of harrowing images that repeated themselves over and over again. She slept only when exhaustion took control.

Rose had no idea how long she remained in the hospital ward. It became her home, despite its bleakness, despite Sister Orta's increasing animosity. It changed from the place she loathed with all her might when she first found herself there, to the place where she found strange comfort in the daily routine that played out around her but left her largely untouched.

As she regained some of her strength, she was made to leave her bed to visit the bathroom. Sometimes, though she was warned not to, she would wander along the grim, grey corridors and peer without much interest into rooms where nurses were gathered or where other patients were being treated. While her bed was being remade, she would sit in the chair at the side and stare at the opposite wall. She made no attempt to look at the books and magazines that one of the young nurses brought her from time to time.

It was a shock, therefore, when one day Sister Orta pulled the curtain round her bed, gave Rose her clothes, freshly washed and ironed, and told her to get herself dressed because the doctors had pronounced her well enough to go home.

But I don't have a home, Rose wanted to protest, and then she wondered if Aunt Mirela and Uncle Aleksandar had come to fetch her at last. *Is it them? Am I going home with them?* She could hardly contain herself in her desire to find out. *I knew they'd find me eventually.*

Early that afternoon, her bed was suddenly surrounded by a group of people and she was lifted into a wheelchair. The woman with the blonde hair and the navy suit, who had already introduced herself as Mrs Luca, fussed over her and tried to hold her hand, her sickly sweet perfume mixing unhappily with the bleached air Rose had grown used to. A tall man with a moustache – her husband – hovered behind the woman, immaculately dressed but curiously hunched, his lips pursed. He looked every-where except at Rose. Rose stared at him and saw that he was supporting himself on a walking stick. *Is he in pain?* she wondered. *Is that why he seems angry?*

Rose quickly understood that she was being taken away from the hospital by Mrs Luca and her husband, though she had no idea why. *Where are Aunt Mirela and Uncle Aleksandar? They need to know what's happening to me. They need to know where to find me!* She had a brief, powerful urge to resist, but in her weakened state she couldn't summon up enough energy. Her fate had been decided for her, and she felt that there was absolutely nothing she could do about it. Sister Orta stood close by, issuing instructions, glad to be rid of such a troublesome patient, Rose could tell.

'We'll be staying in our hotel, just for tonight,' the woman in the suit was saying. 'I've bought you some clothes. Nice clothes. The sort I'd buy my own daughter, Victoria. She can't wait to meet you – I've told her a lot about you.'

'Goodbye, then, child,' said Sister Orta. 'You've certainly landed on your feet and no mistake. Mr and Mrs Luca have been able to arrange papers for you so that you can live with them. Try to return their kindness and stop this stubborn refusal to speak.'

Rose stared at her with loathing. *Have you even tried to find my family?*

'She'll be just fine.' Mrs Luca smiled indulgently at Rose. 'The poor thing has been through such a lot.'

'Spoil her at your peril,' Sister Orta warned. 'Personally, I think what you're doing is madness. We've had her type in here before. They're born trouble.'

'I'll thank you to keep your thoughts to yourself,' Mrs Luca said shortly.

'Can we just get on?' Mr Luca growled at his wife. 'This leg's killing me.'

Mrs Luca signalled to a man in a blue uniform and a peaked cap to take hold of the wheelchair.

Again, Rose wanted to stop what was happening. She leant forward in the chair, trying to stand up, but Mrs Luca took her by the shoulders and eased her back.

'We don't want you falling out.' The woman chuckled nervously. 'You've done yourself enough damage already.'

Rose found herself being wheeled along the grim, grey corridors she knew so well, away from the ward. Mrs Luca tottered alongside in red high heels, while Mr Luca followed behind, huffing and puffing, his walking stick clunking on the concrete floor. When they reached the doors and pushed through to the outside world, Rose flinched as though someone had thrown a punch in her direction, and squeezed her eyes shut.

If only Papa hadn't been so independent. If only he hadn't insisted that we go off on our own after the carnival.

'It's a little bright, isn't it?' said Mrs Luca. 'It must be a bit of a shock for you after spending so long in hospital.'

Rose hoped she would go on to say how long it had been, but Mr Luca interrupted her.

17

'Too hot, if you ask me,' he said. 'Especially if you've got bandages all the way up your leg. Itchy, they are too.'

'We'll soon be on our way home, dear,' said Mrs Luca.

'Not before time.' Her husband snorted. 'I can't wait to get out of this awful place.'

Rose was panic-stricken. *Where are they taking me? Who are these people anyway? Why are they concerning themselves with me?* She didn't even like them, this woman with her saccharine voice, this man with his hostile glare. She wanted to cry out, but couldn't. It was too agonising. She shrank back in the wheelchair as Mrs Luca ordered the chauffeur to make his way across a busy car park.

They stopped by a large black estate car.

'Here we are,' said Mrs Luca. She opened one of the back doors. 'Now, Petr, please lift the child gently on to the back seat.'

Rose thought about beating the chauffeur with her fists as he put his arms round her. She had had enough of being handled by gadje strangers. *Keep away from me!*

'Keep away from gadje,' Nicu had warned her. 'They're different from us. They have their ways and we have ours. The two don't mix.'

She had never been in a car, however, and curiosity

took over. She had often wondered what it would feel like to sit inside and look out as the landscape sped by. For a brief moment, her mind tricked her into thinking she was sitting on the bench of a horse-drawn wagon, but it quickly threw her back to the present, where Mr Luca was groaning loudly as he manoeuvered himself into the front seat and cursed the absence of his own car.

Mrs Luca climbed in next to Rose and patted her on the hand. 'I expect this feels like a big adventure, doesn't it?' she said. 'There's no need to be scared, though.'

Rose bit her lip and felt her stomach lurch as Petr switched on the engine and drove out of the car park. *I don't want to be in here.* Fear took over from curiosity. *Let me out!* She turned to Mrs Luca and noticed that she, too, looked anxious. Her new guardian forced a smile when she saw Rose's face and began a running commentary about the sights they were passing. Rose turned back to the window and gazed at the people going about their business; some were striding purposefully in smart suits, briefcases in hand, others were strolling casually in the warm sunshine, stopping to gaze at grandiose buildings or to peer into shop windows filled with glamorous fashions and glitzy items for the home. None of them would have cared that she was being taken away against her will.

Where is this place? Rose wondered as they crossed a bridge over a wide and winding river.

'We come back here every year,' she heard Mrs Luca saying. 'It's our favourite city in the world. It's a pity it has one of the worst hospitals in the country, but we weren't able to move you to a better one.'

Rose knew of the big cities in her country, but she had no idea which one this was.

'Have you been here before?' Mrs Luca asked.

Rose shook her head. They had travelled through small towns, but her father preferred to take a long route rather than attempt to ride through a city.

'Cities aren't for the likes of us,' he used to say. 'You can lose your soul in a city. In fact, you can lose your *life* in a city and nobody would care.'

Her mother had laughed and told him he exaggerated. 'People are people,' she said. 'We're lucky we have such freedom, but not everyone is so lucky. If you're forced to live like a caged animal, you might behave like a caged animal.'

'Ha!' scoffed Nicu. 'People make their own choices.'

People are people. Rose's lips sketched the words, her mother's voice echoing softly from somewhere deep inside.

'Are you trying to speak? Darling, the child is trying to speak!'

Mrs Luca leant over and tried to attract her husband's attention. At the same time, the driver pushed his horn and the car screeched to a halt.

'Idiot!' Mr Luca yelled at the car in front, which had pulled up without warning. He clutched his leg and groaned theatrically.

Mrs Luca slumped back in her seat and let out a low moan. Her hands began to shake uncontrollably. Rose tried not to look at her. She stared out of the window, frightened and puzzled, but relieved that the spotlight had turned away from her. Petr apologised to his employers and accelerated again as the road ahead cleared. They continued in silence.

At last the car turned into a private forecourt.

'Ah, here we are,' Mrs Luca said with forced brightness. She straightened her skirt and sat forward in her seat as the car pulled up outside a tall, glass-fronted building. 'The first stop in our journey home.'

Chapter 5

Home. Rose pondered the meaning of the word as she stretched out on the deep, soft mattress of her temporary bed. Its sumptuous quilt was kicked unceremoniously to the floor. It was too hot in the room! *How do people sleep in such heat?* Mrs Luca had set the temperature before wishing Rose goodnight, kissing her on the forehead and disappearing into her own room next door. Rose grimaced at the thought of the kiss and the waft of sickly perfume that accompanied it. She listened to the low rumble of someone snoring next door that the walls of the prestigious hotel failed to stifle. Sometime earlier, she had heard raised voices, though she couldn't decipher what was being said, nor even what language it was being said in. Silence had fallen briefly, before the rumble had commenced and settled into a rhythm.

Home. Nicu snored. Nicu's snore was elephantine,

especially when he had been drinking his home-brewed ale. In the confines of their wagon, it often woke them up. Esme would dig him hard in the ribs with her elbow or her fist. He would snuffle and snort, then turn over, and for a while peace would follow, until he cranked it up again. Rani thought it was hilarious and mimicked him, though mostly he slept through his father's nocturnal ruckus. Rani could sleep through anything, even thunderstorms. Rose didn't like thunderstorms. No matter how many times Esme told her that she was perfectly safe and that nothing bad was going to happen to her, Rose couldn't help jumping out of her skin at every loud clap of thunder. She was convinced one of the claps would make the wagon explode and that they would all die.

The wagon did explode, but not because of a thunderstorm. It had been their home. The only home she knew. Not a house in the country, with its own piece of land. Not a flat in a town, with windows so thick that they cut out all sounds of life outside. *Why*, Rose wondered, *would anyone want to live in a house or a flat? Why would anyone want to live in a place where you woke up, opened the curtains, and everything around you was the same, day in, day out?* Rose was sure she would die of boredom. She grew impatient when they rented a trailer and stayed put in the same place for a few weeks over the winter. Yet there were children she spoke to in villages where they stopped who were shocked that she was happy to leave her friends behind, that she didn't go to school, that her only permanent home was the wagon.

'But it's tiny!' they said. 'How do you all fit in?'

'It's cosy,' Rose replied. 'And we spend a lot of time outdoors.'

'What about when it's cold?' they asked.

'Who wants to be in a big place when it's cold?' she replied. 'In a small place you can snuggle up together. And we've got a stove. Anyway, we're used to the cold.'

Some of them envied the fact that Rose didn't go to school. Others told her she would never get a good job.

'Why do I need to go to a school to study things like geography and nature and science when it's all around me?' she used to say, quoting Nicu, who was adamant they would learn far more from travelling than sitting in a stuffy classroom.

'I can show you the stars and constellations while we sit by the fire at night,' her father was fond of saying. 'I can show you the tracks made by animals when we forage through the woods for food. I can teach you to recognise birds and their songs when we wake early in the morning to set off for new pastures. I can take you to see mountains and valleys, rivers and seas, forests and grasslands.'

Rose loved it when Nicu spoke like that, his voice strong and musical, his eyes glinting.

'Your father is a man of poetry and passion,' Esme always said. 'And that's why I married him.'

Home. Home is where you feel safe and loved and secure, Rose concluded. It's where you are surrounded by people who mean more to you than anything else in the world and by things that you cherish because they are part of your history and part of your story. *Papa would have been proud of me for coming up with such a description*, Rose thought to herself. She knew that he might have said something similar once upon a time in his strong, musical voice.

Alone now in the darkness of a hotel room, she cried for the home she had lost. For Nicu, for Esme and for Rani. For her history and for her story. Next door the rumble continued, persistent and heedless.

Chapter 6

Rose was woken by a loud knocking. She had no idea where she was or what time of day it was.

A door opened, thrusting light across her, and an overly cheerful voice announced, 'Time to wake up, child. We need to be at the airport in an hour.'

Mrs Luca placed a tray on the bedside table and opened the curtains.

'I hope you slept well,' she said, disappearing through the door to re-emerge with an armful of clothes, which she laid on the bed. 'Eat your breakfast, then get yourself dressed.'

Rose pulled herself up in the bed, while the woman plumped up the pillows behind her before placing the tray on her lap.

'Bon appétit. Now, don't you be long. It's a beautiful day – a perfect day for going home.'

Rose waited until Mrs Luca had gone back to her own room to lift the silver lid that covered her breakfast. Underneath was a plate piled high with slices of cold meat, cheese, tomato and pickles. In a basket with a white napkin across the top were four different kinds of rolls, and in another, smaller basket were six tiny pots of jam. A bowl decorated with pink flowers contained a large pat of butter. Rose couldn't help but gape. *Is this all for me?* She waited to see if Mrs Luca was coming back to join her, but the clatter of knives and forks next door told her that Mr and Mrs Luca had their own trays.

After endless bland and repetitive hospital food, Rose tucked in. Her first mouthful of salami sent a thousand taste buds into fits of delight, calmed only by the soft creaminess of one of the four cheeses, before being tickled again by the cool, sweet tang of ripe tomato and the sharp contrast of the pickles. She plucked one of the rolls from its nest. It was still warm and quickly soaked up the lashings of butter she gave it. She chose damson jam to go on top, only to be disappointed because it had none of the rich flavour of Esme's home-made version.

Rose pushed the roll aside, her appetite spoiled in an instant by the memory of the smell of damsons, sloes or blackberries boiling away in the iron pot on their stove. She had loved it when they stopped the wagon in the middle of nowhere to scour the hedgerows for fruit. While Nicu stayed behind to check the wheels of the wagon, or to feed the horse, Philippos, or simply to smoke his pipe in peace, Esme led her and Rani away like troops on a mission. Rani wore his bowl on his head and marched purposefully in front of his mother and sister. He and Rose picked everything they could find among the lower branches of bushes and trees. Occasionally, they stopped to play hide-and-seek, especially in fields where the grass was long, or in shallow woodland, where there were plenty of trees to hide behind. Rani lost interest in collecting fruit sooner than she did, though he was quick enough to demand his share of the spoils when they returned to the wagon and Esme produced her delicious puddings.

Rose missed her little brother with a sharp pang of sadness. He was five years younger than she was, but he had made her laugh with his antics and the way he sometimes ran their mother ragged. He was always disappearing when it was time for his wash, and Esme could never find her cooking pots because he took them to collect beetles or slow-worms or frogs in.

Rose put the tray on the bed and slid out from underneath the covers. She was anxious to get dressed before Mrs Luca started to fuss over her. She took the clothes, locked herself in the bathroom, put them on and stood in front of the full-length mirror. She didn't recognise the girl who stood before her. This girl was so thin! Her face was gaunt and pale. Her eyes were dull, her hair lifeless. She looked so much older, especially in the neat skirt and blouse, the white socks and shiny black shoes.

Is that really me?

She sat down on the toilet seat, feeling utterly exhausted.

'It will take you a while to get your strength back, though you've mended well,' Sister Orta had told her. 'You were very seriously injured, so don't go thinking you'll be able to run around like other children until a good few months from now.'

There was a tap on the bathroom door.

'Are you all right, child?' an anxious voice asked.

Am I all right? Rose asked herself silently.

'It's time we were going. We don't want to miss our flight, do we?'

Rose stood up and looked in the mirror again. She nodded her head slowly, then more quickly.

'Will you come out now, child?'

'What's she doing in there?' Another voice. Mr Luca.

29

Impatient. 'She'll make us late at this rate. I don't know why we're bothering.'

'You know why we're bothering. It's the least we can do. Please, child, come out now.'

Rose waited a few more moments before opening the door.

'There,' said Mrs Luca. 'Don't you look nice? Just let me tidy your hair and then you'll look as pretty as a picture.'

Mr Luca tutted loudly as Mrs Luca fetched a brush, and more loudly still as she fiddled with Rose's hair.

'That's it. All done.' She stood back and admired her handiwork. 'Perfect,' she said.

'For goodness' sake, can we get a move on now?' growled Mr Luca.

'We couldn't let the child go out looking as if she had just got out of bed, could we?'

'I don't care if she resembles the back end of a donkey, as long as we catch our flight. And when are you going to stop calling her "child" and tell her her name?'

The fixed smile dropped from Mrs Luca's face. 'Shhh!' she hissed.

'No, I won't shush,' snapped Mr Luca. 'She needs to know before we reach the airport, before they check her papers. She could make it very difficult for us.'

Rose stared at Mrs Luca, who looked alarmed.

'I . . . we . . .' Mrs Luca began. 'We don't know your name. We can't keep calling you "child", can we? It's not very friendly. Until you can tell us your real name, we've decided to call you Anna. We think Anna is a nice name. What do you think?'

Rose continued to stare at her, unable to take in what she was saying.

'So your name is Anna Luca,' Mrs Luca said, smiling again now. 'My husband is called George and I'm Daphne.'

Chapter 7

Rose gazed all around her as Petr wheeled her through the revolving doors into the airport. There were so many people, some of them hurrying, some lounging on seats, some standing idly in long queues, their luggage piled high in trolleys alongside.

'Have you ever been on a plane before, Anna?' Mrs Luca asked her.

Rose shook her head.

'There's nothing to be frightened of,' Mrs Luca continued. 'Much safer than cars.' As soon as she'd said it, however, she looked perturbed and hurried ahead with her husband to find their check-in desk.

Rose was petrified. It hit her that she was leaving her country, leaving her people, leaving everything she had ever known. Leaving her family and friends. Where were they? Why hadn't they come to find her? Why hadn't she told Sister Orta about Aunt Mirela and Uncle Aleksandar? She could tell the Lucas now. It wasn't too late. She could tell George and Daphne that she couldn't, wouldn't go with them. *And if they won't listen I'll shout out loud until someone comes to help me.*

She shifted forward in the wheelchair and tried to stand up. Petr caught her and gently pulled her back down. She turned towards him and he smiled at her awkwardly. She tried to say something, but it was futile. She couldn't bring herself to speak, however much it might change the course of events. Her voice was locked up inside, in a place which she dared not enter. Tears rolled silently down her cheeks. She brushed them angrily away when she saw Mr and Mrs Luca returning. She vowed to herself that they would never see her cry. She didn't want Mrs Luca's suffocating concern and she certainly didn't want Mr Luca's scowling contempt. It was clear he had something against her and was giving in to his wife's wishes to provide a home for her.

Why? Rose wondered. *Why have they suddenly appeared in my life and taken charge of me? Why is Mrs Luca so determined to care for me as if I'm her own daughter?*

She stared at her now – the face with its excess of make-up, the bleached hair with its dark roots showing, the close-fitting suit, the high heels clicking inexorably towards her, the forced smile as she caught Rose's stare.

'We're being fast-tracked through because of your condition,' she said. 'Isn't that good? Not that there's much of a queue for first class, of course.' She was talking very quickly and sounded anxious.

Rose had no idea what she meant but gave a brief nod. She felt sorry momentarily for this woman with her bad-tempered husband.

They said goodbye to Petr and made their way to have their papers and baggage checked. Mrs Luca placed her hand on the back of Rose's head and tried to look relaxed, while Mr Luca wiped sweat from his forehead and demanded that the attendant let them through speedily because his daughter needed the toilet. They both seemed relieved when their papers were handed back to them and the check-in attendant wished them a good flight.

Mrs Luca wheeled Rose to a window so that she could watch the planes taking off and landing. Rose had always wondered how a machine so big and heavy could stay up in the air. The thought of being inside one absolutely terrified her. At the same time, she was fascinated to know what the world would look like from high above, to know what it would be like to fly through the clouds. She started as a huge plane decorated with the flag of her country left the runway. For a brief moment, it felt as though her country was abandoning her. She raised her hand as if to pull it back, but dropped it again quickly.

'Not long now, Anna,' said Mrs Luca. 'I expect this will be the most exciting thing you've ever done. I know it was when I first flew. Of course, we fly all the time now.'

'The hanging about never gets any better,' grumbled Mr Luca.

'At least we can be grateful that our flight's on time,' replied Mrs Luca. 'The worst thing is when it's delayed for hours.'

The knot of anxiety in Rose's stomach began to tighten. Was it too late to resist what was happening? Could she try again to find a voice to tell people that she was being taken away against her will?

'This leg's giving me agony again,' Mr Luca moaned. 'It's going to be a nightmare on the plane.'

'No worse than it will be for Anna,' said his wife, without looking at him.

'Don't make such crass comparisons, Daphne. She's young, she can adapt. If you keep fussing over her she'll wind up as spoilt as Victoria.'

'I'm not fussing, George. Can't you see the poor thing is anxious? And so would you be if you hadn't flown before.'

'You don't know that she hasn't flown before. You don't know anything about her. She could be a murderess for all you know.'

'Now you're being ridiculous. Does she look like a murderess?'

'I don't know what a murderess looks like, and neither do you.'

Mrs Luca rolled her eyes. 'She's only a child. And you would know more about murder than she does,' she muttered.

'What was that?' Mr Luca demanded, but he was interrupted by the loudspeaker.

'Our flight's being called,' Mrs Luca said quickly. She didn't wait for her husband to reply, but began to push Rose along a wide corridor. 'I'm dying to show you the house and the garden, and for you to meet Victoria, and the dog, Crumble. He's such a fun dog. A pedigree Norfolk terrier. Think of it – three hours on a plane and then you'll be at the beginning of a brand new life.' She squeezed Rose's shoulder. 'We'll be just fine together, won't we?'

She wasn't expecting a response, and Rose didn't give one.

They reached the departure gate and were called to board the plane ahead of the other passengers. Rose felt as if all eyes were on her as she was helped from her wheelchair by two flight attendants, who guided her down a long, cold, metal tunnel. The thought crossed her mind that there might not be an aeroplane at the end and that she might be about to disappear for ever. She was relieved, therefore, when they came to an archway where a smiling woman in a smart uniform greeted her.

'Welcome on board,' she said. 'I'll be looking after you during your flight.'

She ushered them to the front of the plane and helped Rose into a seat that Rose thought was more like an armchair. Mrs Luca settled next to her, while her husband sat across the aisle. Rose was surprised at how big the cabin was, and was more convinced than ever that it would be impossible for the plane to leave the ground. Other passengers were filing in and being shepherded to their places. They all seemed perfectly calm to Rose as they chatted and made themselves comfortable, opening up books and magazines, or resting their heads and closing their eyes.

'Let me do your belt for you,' said Mrs Luca. She leant over and fitted two straps together round Rose's waist. Rose immediately wanted to undo them and jump up, but Mrs Luca explained that everyone had to wear a seat belt while the plane took off. 'Just in case it's bumpy. We don't want you falling out, do we?' She laughed loudly, failing to realise that it was the second time she had made the same joke.

Rose held on to the arms of her seat and listened intently when one of the cabin crew explained what to do in case of an emergency. It was a lot to take in. She was sure she would forget how to inflate her life jacket, even if she were able to find it under her seat.

And then the engines roared into life. Rose felt her heart hammering inside her chest as if it were trying to get out. Her stomach lurched with the sudden backward movement of the plane. *Why is it going backwards?* When Mrs Luca took hold of her hand and squeezed it tightly, Rose didn't resist.

The plane swung slowly round and began to move forward. Rose dared herself to look out of the window. They were passing by a line of stationary planes, their noses locked into the building Rose's plane was leaving behind. In between were wagons piled high with luggage, forklift trucks shifting boxes, and various security vehicles with lights flashing. Now the plane, still moving slowly, was leaving them all behind.

'We'll finish taxiing in a minute and then prepare for

take-off,' said Mrs Luca, breaking through Rose's thoughts.

Rose could see the runway stretching away into the distance, bordered on either side by grass. Something moved in the grass. It was a rabbit. Rose gasped when she saw it. The rabbit was close to the runway where the plane was heading. Nicu used to shoot rabbits and Esme used to make the most delicious stews with them. But this rabbit lived in the most dangerous place Rose could think of, and she wanted it to survive more than anything else. She willed it to stay in the grass as the plane drew closer then stopped, like a huge monster casually eyeing up its prey, waiting to pounce.

The plane's engines accelerated, the noise becoming almost unbearable. Rose watched the rabbit tear away through the grass. *If only I could do the same*, she thought. Mrs Luca gripped her arm. She tried to free herself, but the grip became tighter. She fixed her gaze back on the window. The plane began to rumble along the runway, faster and faster, shaking furiously, until with one scarcely noticeable movement it left the ground and Rose could see the airport buildings below and small clouds scudding by.

'I hate that bit,' said Mrs Luca.

'I hate you,' Rose mouthed, unseen.

Chapter 8

Somehow, Rose slept through most of the flight. She had been surprised by how smooth it was. Once they were up in the air, it didn't seem as if they were moving at all and she had begun to relax a little. It was bumpier in their wagon when they were on the road, especially if one of the wheels hit a pothole, which happened quite often.

Mrs Luca sprang to life as soon as the plane straightened up and the seat belt signs had gone off. She tried to placate her husband, who complained over and over that it was impossible to get comfortable. He demanded to be given a drink the minute the cabin crew became active after take-off, and grumbled about the meal that was served. When he dropped off to sleep, Mrs Luca turned her attention back to Rose, leaning across her to point out mountains and marvel at the clouds, and chattering continuously about countries they had visited, their home in England and what they would do when they arrived. The more Rose failed to respond, the more she talked, as though desperate to fill the void. Rose closed her eyes in the hope that she would leave her in peace, and found herself drifting off, unable to resist the gentle drone and the almost imperceptible, soothing motion of the plane.

When she woke up, it was to discover that the flight was almost over.

'You had a good sleep,' said Mrs Luca. 'It's only twenty minutes now till we land.'

Rose scowled and stared out of the window. She was astonished at how many houses she could see below, row upon row of them, and a maze of roads with cars beetling along. So many cars! In the distance there were fields – green, manicured fields with sheep and cows dotted about. She followed the meandering trail of a river, and remembered how she used to go paddling with Rani whenever Nicu stopped the wagon by a waterway. Nicu loved to fish and would settle down on the bank some distance away from them, so that their shrieks of laughter and the maelstrom they created when they played wouldn't disturb his musing, or ruin his chance of catching their supper. Once, Rose recalled, Rani had filled a bowl with water, crept along the riverbank and tipped it over Nicu's head. Rose had laughed until her sides ached at the look of shock on her father's face.

She wondered what Victoria would be like. *I bet she won't be fun like Rani. I bet she won't want to play with me.*

A sudden juddering bump and a deafening whoosh of engine noise blew Rose's memories to pieces. She tried to get out of her seat, but was held back by the belt. She was certain the plane was going to explode, that she was going to die. *Why is everyone just sitting there? Why don't they do something?*

She turned to her guardian just as the noise cut out and the plane slowed right down, taxiing to a halt.

Mrs Luca opened her eyes and clapped her hands. 'That was a good landing, wasn't it?' she said.

Rose hardly dared look out of the window again, so afraid was she of the unfamiliar things she might be confronted with. When she did, she saw the runway and alongside it a wide stretch of grass. It was so like the runway she had left behind, she half expected to see the rabbit. She gazed long and hard, willing it to appear, but it didn't.

'Let me help you take your belt off, Anna,' said Mrs Luca, leaning across and fiddling with it.

Rose pushed her hands away yet again and opened the catch herself.

'I'm glad to see you're being independent.' Mrs Luca said graciously. 'We'll soon have you fit and well, then you'll be able to do everything for yourself. I know how tedious it is having to rely on everyone else to do things for you.'

As they made their way off the plane, Mrs Luca turned to her again. 'Welcome to England, Anna,' she said.

This is it, then. Rose grimaced. *Nobody even knows I exist any more.*

Chapter 9

Rose couldn't believe her eyes when the chauffeur-driven car they had hired drew up in front of a pair of high wooden gates, which opened as if by magic to let them through. On the other side, a long, yellow gravel drive – seemingly almost as long as the airport runway – stretched ahead of them, ending in a circular sweep around a fountain shaped like a whale, its open mouth gushing out water. The house at the top of the drive was so big that Rose thought it must be a hotel.

'At last,' said Mrs Luca. 'Welcome to your new home, Anna. I can't wait to show you around.'

'Never mind that,' said her husband. 'Let's just get inside and have Marina run a bath for me. This leg's killing me.'

'Think how much worse it would be if we weren't able to travel first class,' observed Mrs Luca.

'What do I care how much worse it might have been?' growled Mr Luca.

'Anna's not making a fuss and I'm sure she couldn't have been comfortable,' Mrs Luca continued.

'I wish you'd stop these pointless comparisons,' Mr Luca snapped at her. 'She's a child. It's easier for her.'

He pushed open the door of the car and ordered the driver to help him out. At the same time, the door of the house opened. A young woman in a grey uniform appeared.

'Ah, Marina,' Mrs Luca called. 'Come and give Anna a hand, will you?'

Marina hurried down the steps and came towards them.

'Welcome back, sir, ma'am,' she said. 'We've missed you.'

'It's good to be back,' said Mrs Luca. 'And this is Anna, the young girl I told you about. Help her into the house, would you?'

Marina smiled at Rose. 'Take my arm, miss,' she said. 'I can take your weight.'

Rose shook her head. *I can stand on my own two feet. I've had enough of being treated like an invalid.*

'Don't be stubborn, Anna, please.' Mrs Luca intervened.

Just at that moment, though, a tall, fair-haired girl,

several years older than Rose, ran from the house and towards the car.

'Daddy! Mummy!' she cried. 'You're back! I've been so worried about you.' She threw herself into her father's arms. 'Poor Daddy,' she said. 'How's your poor leggy?'

'It's been a nightmare, darling. A double break and muscle damage, according to the medics, but I'm sure it'll mend more quickly now I'm here.'

'I hope they've thrown the other driver in prison,' said the girl. 'And how are you, Mummy?'

'I'm fine, darling. A few bumps and bruises, but nothing serious. Now, let me introduce you to Anna. Anna, this is our daughter, Victoria.'

The girl stared hard at Rose, then shrugged. 'I still don't know why you had to bring her here,' she muttered.

She turned her back and continued in a language that Rose didn't understand, her voice tight and harsh. Mrs Luca responded in the same language, her tone light and placatory. She attempted to take her daughter's arm, but the girl pulled away and slipped her arm through her father's instead. The two of them walked towards the house, sending the woman in grey ahead of them to make a pot of tea, leaving Mrs Luca to shepherd Rose while the chauffeur brought their luggage.

'My daughter's a little overwrought,' Mrs Luca explained to Rose. 'The poor child has had to cope without us for three months and she's very emotional.'

Rose watched the girl as she walked ahead of them and took an instant dislike to her. She had an arrogance, a self-assurance that showed itself in the swaying of her hips and the tossing of her hair. She was slim, her long limbs bare and brown. She was wearing a lacy white blouse and a pair of pink shorts pulled in at the waist by a silver belt. Nicu would have told her to cover herself up, that she was exposing too much flesh. Once or twice, she peered round at Rose with a look of sheer disdain, before pulling her father closer to her in a statement of possession.

Rose was used to such looks. She was a Roma, after all. They had long since ceased to bother her. Esme and Nicu had taught her to expect far more than disdain from the gadje, or non-Roma.

'Simmering hatred is what we get from a lot of people. We might just as well be vermin the way they feel about us,' Nicu used to say. 'They don't know anything about who we are individually, they just judge us as a group.'

'Some of our kind deserve their bad reputation,' Esme would occasionally respond to Nicu's rantings. 'There are rotten apples in every basket and they spoil it for the rest of us.'

'There are plenty of rotten apples among the gadje. We don't judge all of them by that.'

The truth was that they kept away from the gadje as much as possible.

'We've been shoved from place to place, from country to country, ever since time began,' Nicu often told his family. 'We're outsiders. We don't fit in because we don't lead our lives the way the gadje think we should. As if there's only one way.'

Rose felt a shock of unease as she approached the front door of the Lucas' home. She was entering enemy territory. It had been bad enough sitting with them on the plane and in the car. Now she was going to live with them. Her family would have been horrified. She hesitated on the doorstep as Mrs Luca took her elbow and ushered her in, and wondered whether anyone would chase after her if she tried to run away.

'Don't be shy, Anna. You're with friends here. You'll soon feel at home and then I'm sure you'll find your voice again. I can't wait for that moment. We'll have to have a celebration when it happens.'

Mrs Luca pushed her forward into a huge hallway, where a wide central staircase ascended from a marble floor and was flanked on either side above by a galleried landing. There were so many doors leading off the

48

hallway and the landing that Rose wondered where they could possibly all lead and how many people lived behind them. It was like something from a film she had once seen on Uncle Aleksandar's television and she half expected all the doors to open at once and a chorus of dancers and singers to appear.

From behind one of the doors on the left she heard the jingle of cutlery, and from close by she heard the voices of Mr Luca and his daughter, followed by peals of laughter. Mrs Luca headed in that direction.

'Come, Anna. We'll have a well-earned cup of tea, then I'll show you around.'

The laughter stopped the minute they crossed the threshold of a large room dominated by a huge open fireplace, whose dark wood surround was ornately decorated with spirals and twists. Mr Luca was sitting in a high-backed leather chair, his daughter perched on one arm with her hand in his.

'Here we are,' said Mrs Luca, smiling happily and striding towards a leather sofa covered with an animal hide. 'Why don't you sit next to me over here?'

Rose heard the words and thought they were aimed at her. As she sat down, she realised that Mrs Luca had in fact been looking at Victoria when she said them. However, Victoria made no attempt to change places and her mother quickly concealed her disappointment by pretending that she had meant Rose all along.

An awkward silence descended. It was broken when Mr Luca tutted loudly and tapped on his watch.

'Shall I go and hurry her up, Daddy?' Victoria asked.

'I'm sure she's doing her best,' said Mrs Luca. 'How have you been coping without us, darling? How's your schoolwork?'

'Boring, boring, boring,' said Victoria. 'What's the point of learning Latin when nobody speaks it any more?'

'There's plenty of point and we've been through this before. Latin is the root of many other languages and many everyday words derive from it,' Mrs Luca replied.

'So what? Who needs to know where words come from?' Victoria retorted.

'You might as well say there's no point in learning history since it's all about things that have happened in the past and can't be revisited,' argued Mrs Luca.

'There *isn't* any point in learning history, except perhaps what happened a few years ago,' said Victoria.

'But history is what has shaped who we are,' Mrs Luca disagreed.

'Far better to learn about business and finance, I say,' interjected Mr Luca, just as Marina appeared with a tray of tea and biscuits. 'This house wasn't bought on history and Latin.'

'What do you think, Anna?' Victoria suddenly addressed her. 'Do you think history and Latin are a waste of time?'

Rose could feel herself blushing with confusion and looked to Mrs Luca for help.

'How would you like your tea, Anna? With milk? Sugar?' Mrs Luca picked up the plate of biscuits and offered it to Rose. Rose nodded in response to both questions and took three biscuits from the plate. She was hungry, despite the enormous breakfast she had eaten that morning.

Victoria immediately gasped, then snorted with derision. 'She's taken three in one go, Mummy!' She turned to her father and said something to him that Rose didn't understand.

'The poor girl's hungry!' Mrs Luca defended Rose. 'As you would be if you'd been living on hospital meals for weeks on end. And I won't have you talking in English in front of her, thank you, Victoria. Not until she learns how to speak it herself.'

'But she can't speak at all, Mummy.' Victoria pouted.

'You know what I mean, and she can understand our own language perfectly well.'

Again, Victoria muttered something to her father, who grunted and demanded his tea.

Rose was amazed that the tea was being served from a silver pot and that the sugar and milk were also in silver containers. She balanced her cup and saucer on her knee, terrified she might spill something on the pale, patterned carpet. She hardly dared lift a biscuit to her mouth in case it caused Victoria more mirth, and wondered if she should put two of them back on the plate instead of leaving them to stare at her accusingly from her saucer.

She was relieved when Mr Luca finished his tea and stood up.

'I shall have my bath and then I expect to be left in peace for the rest of the day,' he announced, before walking stiffly out of the room.

Victoria jumped to her feet. 'I'm going for a ride,' she said abruptly.

'Oh, but, darling, I was looking forward to having a catch-up with you,' protested Mrs Luca. 'It's been so long since we were together.'

'Later,' said Victoria. 'Anyway, you've got *her* to keep you company.'

Chapter 10

Rose lay among the plumped-up pillows of her enormous bed and listened in the pitch-black silence. Heavy curtains at the windows prevented even the smallest glimmer of light from entering the room, making it difficult for her to tell what time it was. She had tried to sleep, turning from one side to the other, pushing back the thick, quilted covers because she was too hot, then pulling them over herself again because she was cold. After Mrs Luca had pecked her on the cheek and said her goodnights, and before settling down, Rose had tiptoed to the bedroom door to see if she could lock it, and had been disappointed to find that there was no key. She didn't like being shut in, but she wanted to keep everyone else out.

She thought about the events of the last two days. They felt like the longest two days of her life. Only the previous morning she had woken in her hard, narrow, starched hospital bed, surrounded by the familiar sounds and smells of sickness and suffering, but comfortable in the cocoon she had built around herself. Since then, she had flown across the world into the chilly, privileged lives of a family who might just as well have come from outer space for all that they bore any relation to Rose's own family, and where unfettered luxury threatened to smother her. *I'd give anything to be snuggled up at the back of the wagon or camped underneath the stars.*

Rose clambered out of bed, crept over to the windows and peered through the curtains. She gazed up at the sky, but there were no stars. The moon was just visible through a sweep of cloud and picked out the tops of trees with thin shafts of light. There was a spill of light too on the water spurting from the whale fountain, which made it look as though it was dancing on hot coals. Rose opened a window slowly, carefully, wanting to breathe the night air and hear the night sounds. The gentle flurry of a breeze greeted her, still mild but with a cool edge that made her shiver. Somewhere in the distance a tawny owl hooted, and closer by a vixen screeched.

The crunch of gravel made Rose pull back sharply. She leant forward again slowly, screening herself with the curtain, and stared down. A tiny red glow hovered in the darkness, disappeared, flickered, then disappeared again. There was a muffled cough, a further crunch of gravel. The red glow moved agitatedly backwards and forwards, then suddenly the entire area in front of the house was drowned in white light.

'Blast!' Rose heard as she dropped the curtain. 'Wretched lights!'

She stood to the side of the window and moved the curtain just enough to enable her to see who it was. Mr Luca, wearing striped pyjamas, was stalking up and down directly below her. Seconds later, he dropped his cigarette to the ground, trod on it savagely and turned his head up in the direction of Rose's window. He stayed there for a while, staring, before striding back into the house. The security lights stayed on as though expecting this intruder to return, but eventually abandoned their vigil, and the house and grounds were plunged into a deeper blackness as the moon was swallowed up by the clouds.

Rose crept quickly back to bed, heart pounding, legs like jelly. *Did he see me? Is Mr Luca on his way upstairs to ask me why I was spying on him?* She pulled all the bedding right up to her chin and listened for any sound that might warn her he was on his way, wishing again that she had been able to lock the door.

A clock began to chime. *One, two, three*, she counted. *Why was Mr Luca wandering around outside at three o'clock in the morning?* It was sweltering under the covers, but she dared not push them back – not yet, not until she could be sure that nobody was coming.

At last, she decided it was safe to emerge. She pushed the covers away and sat up against the pillows. *I haven't done anything wrong*, she decided. *Why should he be cross with me just because I wasn't asleep?* She had looked out of the window and seen him smoking, that was all. Except that it wasn't all. What she had seen was that he was able to walk perfectly normally – that all the limping and groaning was a sham. *So what?* she thought. *He wants people to feel sorry for him. He wants attention.*

Uncle Aleksandar could be like that, Rose remembered Esme saying. Uncle Aleksandar could describe a minor stomach discomfort as a major digestive problem and have poor Aunt Mirela running around after him with lotions and potions until she was ready to drop, while he, when she wasn't looking, would indulge himself with multiple bars of chocolate and too much home-brewed ale. He loved the attention and sympathy his wife gave him, but Esme said that Aunt Mirela knew exactly what he was about and didn't mind playing the game with him.

'She loves him, that's the fact of it,' said Esme. 'She'll do anything for him. And if he makes a song and dance about things from time to time, so what?'

Rose found it easy to understand why Aunt Mirela loved him. Uncle Aleksandar was big and loud and funny and full of beans – at least when he wasn't full of ale, which tended to make him soppy. He played the cello to Nicu's violin, and what he lacked in talent he made up for in melodrama. During ballads he swayed from side to side, drawing his bow across the strings with exaggerated sweeps and pulling such sad faces that he looked as if he would dissolve into tears, which indeed he seemed to when, at the end, he wiped a handkerchief across his brow and dabbed at his eyes. During jigs and reels he rocked on his seat and tapped his feet, nodding his head furiously at the same time and grinning from ear to ear. He couldn't sing, though occasionally he tried to join in, until Nicu shot him a warning look, but he still hummed and whistled and clicked his tongue.

He was a boxer too, one of the best in his day, Esme told her, before his waistline gave in to his appetite. He still liked to think he could hold his own against the young pretenders who wanted to challenge him, but Aunt Mirela protected him by sending them away.

'We all know you were the best,' she tutted. 'You

57

don't have to keep proving it. And you know if you do insist you'll be laid up for days.'

'I could whip the pants off any of those whipper-snappers,' Uncle Aleksandar snorted, jumping from his seat and throwing punches at the air. But his protests were hollow. He quickly settled back down to whittling wood or swapping channels on his treasured television.

Aunt Mirela certainly loved him, and he loved her too. Just as Esme and Nicu had loved each other. Rose was convinced that Mr Luca didn't love his wife, and she couldn't understand how his wife could possibly love him. She had never met anyone so disagreeable, nor anyone who so shamelessly used and abused people.

He had hidden himself away for the remainder of the afternoon, catching up on business matters, he said, until dinner was served, when he complained about the food being too salty and cold. The only person who seemed to escape his ill humour was his daughter. She indulged him nauseatingly and was indulged in return.

Mrs Luca had spent the afternoon slowly showing Rose around the house and gardens, saying, 'We'll take it very steadily, and you must let me know if it's too tiring for you. We can't have you overdoing things the minute you arrive.'

Rose was flabbergasted that one family could live all alone in such an abundance of wealth and space, and wondered why they needed so many rooms for themselves. When she was shown to her own room, she could only stand in the doorway and stare. The bed was big enough for six people! There was a dressing table with three mirrors, and several brushes and combs were laid out on its ornate top. There was an armchair that looked far too decorative to sit on, and a huge wardrobe and chest of drawers for her to keep her clothes in.

'We'll go shopping as soon as you feel strong enough and fill them up for you,' Mrs Luca suggested. 'I'm sure you'd like that, wouldn't you? And Victoria can come with us to help choose. Victoria knows what young people are wearing at the moment. We don't want you to look out of place, do we?'

She patted the bed and indicated that Rose should sit down with her. Rose did as she was asked, perching uncomfortably on the edge.

'We want you to be happy here, Anna,' Mrs Luca said. 'We want you to think of us as your family. I know it will be hard for you at first, but I hope that in time . . . We can't replace your real family, of course, but we'll do our best to make you feel at home.' She gazed at

Rose. 'Can you say something, Anna? Can you tell me how you feel?'

Rose was shocked. The direct question took her aback, plunging her into turmoil. She got up from the bed and stood helplessly in the middle of the room, pushing her fist against her mouth. Mrs Luca came up to her and tried to hug her.

'I'm so sorry,' she said. 'That was foolish of me. I won't ask you again. You don't have to talk until you're ready.'

A noise behind them made them both turn.

Victoria was hovering in the doorway. She cleared her throat and said, 'Is it my turn to have some time with you now, Mummy?' She looked Rose up and down. 'You'll be all right on your own for a bit, won't you?'

Rose nodded, more than grateful for the suggestion.

'Of course, darling. I'm coming now,' Mrs Luca gushed. 'Why don't you put your things away and have a rest before dinner, Anna?'

Rose nodded again and watched them leave. As they did, she heard Victoria say to her mother, 'She's not another of your projects, is she, Mummy? She looks like a Gypsy to me.'

Chapter 11

The one thing that excited Rose about her tour of the Lucas' estate was the stable yard and horses. She had grown up with horses and had learnt to ride at a very young age, cradled at first between Nicu's powerful arms, then taking off on her own as soon as she was strong enough to grip with her legs. Philippos was a gentle giant of a horse, who had been with the family since Rose was three and could only manage to call him Peepops.

One day, Esme told her that 'Philippos' meant 'friend of horses'. Rose thought this was hilarious.

'He's a horse!' she cried. 'Of course he's a friend of horses!'

She loved to ride him bareback across fields, galloping through the high grass, and along empty country lanes, lulled by the *clip-clop* of his hooves. There was no feeling like the sense of freedom it gave her, and she knew Philippos loved it too. His head bobbed up and down, his ears were alert and he whinnied softly over and over again.

When he pulled the wagon, he obeyed Nicu's every instruction, tuning in to the sound of his master's voice, happy to be tethered to his family's home. At night, he stood quietly by the side of the wagon, like a sentry on guard, while his family slept.

Philippos was dead. Rose caught a glimpse of his long white mane as he reared and screamed. She blanked her mind.

Mr and Mrs Luca owned ten horses! There were hunters and hacks and cobs of all sizes and colours. Rose was instantly drawn to a chestnut cob and walked over to stroke its flank.

'Do you like to ride?' Mrs Luca asked her.

Rose nodded.

'Then you shall.' Mrs Luca smiled. 'But that horse, Snooty, belongs to Victoria, together with Griffin, the grey she's taken out. What about this one here? He's called Kosta. He's not too big and has a sweet temperament.'

Rose was disappointed when she saw that Mrs Luca was pointing to a piebald pony, and wanted to tell her that she was perfectly capable of riding a much larger horse. She pulled a face, which Mrs Luca took to mean that she thought the pony was too big.

'Or this one, then,' said Mrs Luca, moving to the next box, where another, smaller pony was shaking its head.

Rose shrugged, losing interest, and saw a flash of irritation cross her guardian's face.

'I'm doing my best here, Anna. Try to show some enthusiasm.' Mrs Luca walked purposefully away from the boxes, before turning to say, 'I'll tell you what, you can ride each of the ponies and then make up your mind. Is that all right?'

Rose nodded and made an effort to look pleased.

'As soon as you're stronger, we'll walk you round the yard with them.'

Satisfied that she and Rose were in agreement, she started to head off in the direction of the gardens. They rounded the corner of the stables just as a tall, dark-haired boy was striding towards them. He was carrying a bucket, which caught Mrs Luca on the shin.

'You fool!' she cried, bending down to rub her leg. 'Didn't you see us coming?'

'I'm very sorry, ma'am,' he spluttered. 'No, I didn't see you.'

'Hurry up and get on with your work, then. The ponies both need mucking out.'

'Yes, ma'am. I was about to see to it. It's good to have you back, ma'am.'

'Yes, I'm sure,' replied Mrs Luca.

The boy touched his fingers to his forehead in a vague interpretation of a salute, glanced quickly at Rose and hurried past them.

'Nothing but trouble, that one,' Mrs Luca said to Rose as they proceeded towards the gardens. 'Unless we nag him, nothing gets done. I don't know why we keep him on, except that he has nowhere else to go, and I like to provide work for people from our home country. He came over here with his sister, but she found herself a husband and didn't want him hanging around. I'd rather you didn't mix with him, though. I don't want you mixing with the servants.'

She shot a look at Rose. Rose wasn't sure whether she was expecting an answer or not, but nodded anyway. She had no intention of mixing with a strange boy. She knew too well that her parents wouldn't have approved if she did.

She trailed along beside Mrs Luca, who led her through an area of formal gardens, telling her about all the work she had had done since they moved in eight years before, and pointing out rare and unusual plants she had had flown in from different parts of the world.

The centrepiece was a long, rectangular pond surrounded by a low stone wall, home to numbers of large orange and red-and-white fish.

'The fish are my husband's,' Mrs Luca told Rose. 'They're koi carp. Ugly things, I think, but he's passionate about them. The colours make some of them very valuable. Very valuable indeed.'

Rose peered into the water and was amazed at the size of some of the fish. One came close to the edge, rose to the surface and opened its mouth. Rose smiled. She could see right down its throat.

'It'll suck your finger if you put it in the water,' said Mrs Luca.

Rose didn't think she'd like having her finger sucked and shook her head.

They continued through an archway into a walled kitchen garden, where neat rows of vegetables and herbs were growing. At the far end, a man with long black hair tied back in a ponytail was digging up potatoes.

'Ah, there you are, Goran,' Mrs Luca called. 'How are things?'

'Good day to you, ma'am. I'm delighted to see you back safe and healthy,' replied the gardener. 'The place hasn't been the same without you. And is this the young lady you've rescued?'

'This is Anna. She's come to live with us as one of the family. Are those for our dinner?'

'They certainly are, ma'am. Straight from earth to pot, just as you like them.'

Mrs Luca simpered. 'Goran is an absolute find,' she said to Rose. 'What he can't grow isn't worth growing. We rarely buy vegetables or herbs from the super-market. Our own are far superior.'

Rose remembered how her family used to comb woods, fields and hedgerows for their vegetables, fruit and herbs. She and Rani would pounce with glee when they found a mushroom or blackberries or wild garlic. Her family had earned money by picking peas and beans, and the farmers were always generous enough to let them take some away. One of Rose's favourite jobs was shelling peas, though she would often attract Esme's wrath for pinging the last one from a pod at Rani. Rani was a hopeless shot and rarely managed to hit her back.

'Shall we have peas as well?' Mrs Luca asked.

'If ma'am wants peas, then peas she shall have,' replied Goran. He grinned broadly and, much to Rose's astonish-ment, winked at Mrs Luca, who blushed and turned away.

'We'll be eating early,' she said. 'Be sure to get the vegetables to Marina as soon as possible.' She hurried Rose back through the gardens. 'Goran used to keep

66

the gardens of a government minister back home, but lost his job when the minister lost his. He came to England for a change of life and I found him working in a garden centre. Of course, he jumped at the chance of working here.'

They headed towards the stables. Victoria was there, lifting the saddle from her horse, with Crumble the dog sitting by her feet.

'Did you have a good ride, darling?' Mrs Luca called, a signal for the dog to come rushing over to her, yapping furiously.

'Yes, until some idiot blew his horn and frightened the life out of us,' she replied. 'I could have been thrown off for all he cared.'

'I do wish you'd stick to the paths and fields,' Mrs Luca said, frowning.

'That's for babies and novices,' snorted Victoria, staring directly at Rose. 'I suppose you've already told her she can learn to ride if she wants.'

'I believe Anna has ridden before.'

'Well, she's not having one of my horses. She'll never ride one of my horses.'

Before Mrs Luca could respond, Victoria threw down the saddle, called for Crumble to follow and stalked off towards the house.

Chapter 12

When she woke up, Rose didn't know where she was again, nor what time it was. The room was dark, but a sliver of light from a gap she had left in the curtains told her it was morning. Once she had made sense of her surroundings, she wondered what she was supposed to do. *Should I stay in bed and wait to be told? Or should I get up and go downstairs?*

She could at least find out what sort of day it was, she decided. She crossed to the windows and peered through the curtains. It was pouring with rain – a fine, dense rain that obscured all but the immediate vicinity. Rose remembered what had happened during the night and became anxious about seeing Mr Luca. She resolved to put the moment off for as long as possible and stay in her room until someone came for her.

The house was so quiet. *Is everyone else still sleeping?*

It had never been quiet in the wagon, even when they were deep in the country. There were the cries and scufflings of nocturnal animals. In the early hours of the morning there would be the crow of a cockerel, or jays would drop pine cones on the wagon roof. Nicu's snoring spread intermittently through the night, joined in a chorus by Esme's snuffles and Rani's mumbling. Rose had been so used to it that its absence disturbed her more than the cacophony itself. Esme said that Rose sometimes wailed in her sleep, as though caught up in a terrible dream from which there was no escape. *If I wail in my sleep now*, Rose thought, *it will be because the dream is real.*

A knock at the door sent her scrambling back to bed. She sat up against the pillows as the door opened slowly.

'Miss Anna? Are you awake, Miss Anna?'

Rose nodded in the half-light.

'Ah, there you are, Miss Anna. I've brought your breakfast.'

Marina walked towards her, carrying a tray laden with cups, plates and a big silver dome, like the one in the hotel. She placed it carefully across Rose's lap.

'Ma'am said you need building up, so I've brought you cereal, toast and a full English breakfast. When you've eaten it, ma'am says you're to shower, get dressed, go downstairs, and she'll talk you through the plans for the day. Is that all right, Miss Anna?'

Rose nodded. She watched Marina open the curtains, then go to the chest of drawers and take out some clothes.

'It's going to rain all day today according to the forecast,' Marina said. 'It rains a lot in England, I'm afraid.' She grimaced and added, 'I miss our home country', before bustling out of the room.

For the second time in two days, Rose was bewildered by the amount of food that had been placed in front of her, especially when she discovered what lay under the silver dome. A full English breakfast, it seemed, consisted of eggs, bacon, a strange-looking sausage, tomato, beans and mushrooms. Was she really supposed to eat all of it? She dared not leave any if so. Mrs Luca had insisted that she eat every last morsel at dinner the previous evening, even though she had been given a far bigger portion than Victoria.

She ploughed her way through most of it, but in a moment of rebellion she dropped one of the triangles of toast out of the window, watching it land on the gravel and hoping that an animal would eat it before one of the family found it.

In the bathroom Rose tried to remember how to

operate the shower. She fiddled with the taps and knobs and squealed with fright when water suddenly spurted out of the shower head, lifting it from its mount and spraying the carpeted floor. Rose grabbed at it, but it seemed to have a mind of its own, twisting in her hand and squirting her in the face as well as dousing the wall behind her. She reached across the cubicle to turn off the tap and chose to wash at the basin rather than risk a flood. She picked up a flannel and soap and recalled how Esme would have made sure she scrubbed herself until she was pink and glowing. Esme was a stickler for cleanliness. Rose did her mother proud, before dressing hurriedly and standing in front of the dressing-table mirrors to look at herself again.

She really was so thin! There were dark rings under her eyes, and her hair, normally so thick and wavy, draped mournfully over her sunken cheeks. Worse than that, standing there in the neat pink blouse and dark grey trousers that had been left out for her, she looked like a gadje.

'I'm not a gadje, I'm a Roma,' she mouthed in Romani words.

She was scared she would forget her language and culture, forget how to be a Roma. She wanted to tear off her alien clothes, to knock down the walls of her room and run away before she was sucked too far into gadje ways.

The sound of raised voices broke through her thoughts. She moved to the door and listened. A man was shouting. Rose assumed it was Mr Luca, but couldn't be sure. As much as she didn't want to see him, she was also a little curious about what was happening, apart from the fact that she was expected downstairs. She quietly opened the bedroom door and stood by it, listening. A heated conversation was going on in one of the rooms below. Mr and Mrs Luca were arguing. She would have to wait. She didn't dare descend until they had stopped.

Nicu and Esme hadn't argued often, but Rose and Rani hated it when their parents were at loggerheads. They were both strong characters and neither liked to back down, though mostly it was Nicu who called a halt by going off to smoke his pipe, or simply taking the wind out of Esme's sails by telling her she was gorgeous when she was angry. The rows never lasted long, but when they were at their height, Rose used to lie on her bed and bury her head in the cushions if they were travelling, or go as far from the wagon as possible if they were stationary.

It was different listening to Mr and Mrs Luca rowing.

She didn't care that they didn't get on, but she didn't want to get caught in the crossfire.

When it seemed that peace had settled, she picked up her breakfast tray, crept out of her room and made her way downstairs. As she approached the dining room, she heard Mr Luca say loudly, 'I'm going out and I shan't be back until supper. You and your projects will be the death of me.'

'My latest "project", as you call her, is entirely down to you and your arrogance,' Mrs Luca responded, her voice tight with emotion. 'You and your stupidity, and I'll never forgive you.'

'So you're happy to bankrupt me, are you?' Mr Luca shouted. 'Because I'll be taking you down with me. We were perilously close to tipping over the edge before all this, and all you can do is make things worse.'

He stormed out of the room and tore straight into Rose. She lost her grip on the tray. Plates, cups, cutlery and the silver dome clattered to the floor, together with the remains of her breakfast. Rose stood transfixed as runnels of milk and juice soaked into the carpet.

Mr Luca glared at her. 'Clear it up,' he ordered, then barged past, muttering something in what she took to be English.

Rose bent down to do as she was told, only to hear

Mrs Luca say, 'You should have left it in your room. It's Marina's job to clear away. Leave it and come in here.'

Rose noticed the grim set of her lips. She followed her into the room and waited while Mrs Luca composed herself.

'I trust you slept well?'

Rose nodded.

'And ate well?'

Rose nodded again.

'You must be getting a little tired of having to nod and shake your head all the time.'

Rose lowered her eyes and shifted uncomfortably.

'I'm sorry, that was unkind of me. I mustn't take my frustrations out on you. I'm sure you must have plenty of your own.' Mrs Luca didn't wait for a response, but continued, 'You'll begin your schooling straight away. We have a teacher who comes to the house for Victoria, but she conducts her lessons in English. She will teach you too eventually, but we've decided in the short term to take on a qualified English teacher to help you with the rudiments. You'll need to understand and read the language, even if you can't speak it for the time being.'

Rose stared at Mrs Luca in alarm. It hadn't occurred to her that she would be expected to have lessons. In fact, she hadn't given any thought to how she might spend her days, so much had happened to her in such a short space of time. Now Mrs Luca would discover that she had had very little schooling because of her parents' life on the road, and that she could count, but could barely read or write.

'We need to know what you're thinking to make sure you're happy,' said Mrs Luca, 'so we'll buy some notebooks for you to write things down in, and for your lessons. That way you can let us know if you need anything. You might even want to keep a diary.'

'What are you talking about, Mummy? She's a Gypsy. I bet she can't even write.' Victoria stood in the doorway, arms crossed, a scornful look on her face. 'You can't change who she is just by dressing her in smart clothes.'

'How dare you, Victoria! Don't you ever call Anna a Gypsy again,' Mrs Luca said angrily. 'And this has nothing to do with you.'

'I only live here, that's all! You're supposed to be my mother, but you're only concerned about Anna, or whatever her real name is,' shouted Victoria.

'Darling, you know that's not true, and I'll thank you to treat Anna with respect. She doesn't deserve the cut of your tongue.' Mrs Luca adopted a more conciliatory tone.

'And I don't deserve to be sidelined while you wrap yourself round someone else's child,' retorted Victoria.

'It's not like that, you know it's not. I'll just make sure Anna's settled in, then we'll have some proper time together.'

'You've gone too far this time, Mummy. You know you have, and Daddy thinks so too,' Victoria said coolly, then hurried away.

'I seem to be upsetting everyone today,' Mrs Luca said with a false lightness. 'Things will soon settle down, you'll see, and we'll be one big happy family together.'

Chapter 13

Rose had never been on a shopping spree such as the one Mrs Luca took her on the moment she was fit enough. The only shops she had ever visited were small village stores selling bread and milk or needles and cottons. She always loved looking at the shelves loaded with foodstuffs and the bottles filled with colourful sweets. If she and Rani had been good, Esme allowed them to pick their favourites, and they would watch the shopkeeper unscrew the lids of the bottles, pour some of the sweets out on to a set of scales and tip them carefully into small white bags. Rose could have spent all day in the drapers' shops, where Esme took her to choose materials for her dresses. She liked to run her fingers over the different fabrics, especially the silks and satins.

Mrs Luca, Victoria and Rose drove into a big city and parked in a concrete building full of nothing but cars. Then they walked through some huge glass doors that led into what seemed to Rose like a glass palace full of shops, so brightly lit that it hurt her eyes. Crowds of people bustled about, many loaded down with bags but still searching for more things to buy. Rose had to stop herself gawping as Mrs Luca led her past one shop after another, each with its windows full of goods, while Victoria dragged along behind, not wishing, it seemed, to be associated with either her mother or Rose.

Rose had never seen so many handbags and shoes and dresses and coats and pieces of jewellery and scarves and soaps and creams and books and ornaments. It was as if every single item from every single small shop she had ever been in during her lifetime had been gathered together in one place and magic dust thrown around to make every-thing seem bigger and better and more beautiful. One store was selling nothing but chocolates, some decorated with tiny pink and purple flowers, others individually wrapped in silver and gold, or set in gold boxes tied with gossamer ribbons. How Esme would have loved to go in there! Esme adored chocolate and couldn't resist buying some whenever they went into a village, though she always complained that her waistline was expanding because of it.

Seeing the glint in Rose's eyes, Mrs Luca led her into the store and demanded a chocolate for her to sample.

Rose could have died with embarrassment when the shop assistant held out a small plate with a chocolate sitting in the middle.

'Go on, try it,' urged Mrs Luca.

Rose took the chocolate and bit into it. She didn't enjoy it because everyone was staring at her, but she nodded her head as if to say it was delicious. Encouraged, Mrs Luca ordered a large box to be filled with dark and white chocolates. Rose watched as the assistant picked up one chocolate after another with metal tongs and placed them carefully in the box, before tying a big red bow round it.

'Our treat for later on,' said Mrs Luca.

'I thought you were worried about your weight,' Victoria said scornfully.

'A little chocolate once in a while won't do any harm. Besides, we're celebrating our homecoming.'

Victoria sloped out of the shop. Mrs Luca hurried after and linked arms with her, leaning across to whisper something conspiratorially.

'Don't dally, Anna,' she called back. 'We're nearly at the clothes shop, and Victoria's kindly agreed to help us choose for you. She's such an expert at knowing what looks good and what doesn't, aren't you, darling?'

The way Victoria seemed to feel about her, Rose was

convinced she would choose something monstrous just to spite her. She certainly didn't want to wind up in skimpy shorts.

She followed them through a revolving glass door that opened up into a huge store, where the walls were lined on all sides by photographs of models sporting the latest fashions. Underneath were row upon row of shelves piled high with T-shirts and jumpers. The central area was filled with clothing rails neatly arranged in squares, each square surrounding a mannequin perched on a plinth. Trousers, skirts and blouses hung from the lower rails, dresses from those that were higher.

The clothes all seemed to be the same sort of colours, Rose noticed. There were purples and deep reds and black, but no yellows and greens and blues. They looked drab! She was relieved when Mrs Luca led her through an archway into a second hall, where 'the little kids' clothes', as Victoria put it, were on display, and where the colours were brighter.

'Here we are,' said Mrs Luca. 'Where would you like to start, Anna?'

Rose gazed around. She hadn't the slightest idea.

'We'll look at blouses first, then,' said Mrs Luca. 'Four or five should keep you going for the time being.'

'She'll have to have a couple of white ones,' said

Victoria, 'and this blue denim is really cool. And what about this? I wouldn't mind this myself.'

She held up a red-and-white striped blouse with a white collar and cuffs. Rose hated it. *It's more like a man's shirt*, she thought.

'Try it on, Anna,' Mrs Luca suggested. 'Go to the changing room and help her, Victoria.'

Rose shook her head. She didn't want to try on the blouse or any other clothes. She didn't want to stand in front of a mirror and look at herself. She didn't want these strangers staring at her and deciding what she should wear.

'That's not very grateful, is it, Mummy?' Victoria scoffed.

'Don't you like it, Anna?' Mrs Luca asked. 'You choose something, then.'

Rose fixed her eyes on the floor. She had no idea what to choose and was sure that if she did take something from a rail, Victoria would laugh at her choice.

Mrs Luca called a shop assistant and spoke to her in English, pointing to Rose and explaining what they wanted.

When the assistant went away to fetch some items of clothing, Rose overheard Victoria hiss at her mother, 'Don't call her your daughter. She's not your daughter.'

'It's easier that way,' Mrs Luca replied.

'*Don't call me your daughter,*' Rose wanted to say. '*I'm not your daughter. I'm Esme's daughter.*'

The shop assistant returned with arms full of clothes. She held them up in turn for Rose's approval. Rose nodded at every single one of them. She didn't care, as long as she didn't have to try anything on and as long as she could get out of the store without further embarrassment.

'We'll just have to hope they fit you if you really won't try them on,' said Mrs Luca, while the shop assistant folded their purchases and put them into large plastic carrier bags.

'She'll only have herself to blame if they don't,' said Victoria.

She disappeared into the first hall, and by the time Rose and Mrs Luca went back through, she had already picked out two blouses and two jumpers that she wanted her mother to buy her.

'It's only fair,' she said, 'and you promised if I helped Anna I could have something too.'

'Just don't tell your father, that's all,' sighed Mrs Luca. 'Things are a little tight at the moment.'

'Daddy won't mind,' Victoria replied, and plucked a necklace from a stand to add to her selection, despite her mother's protestations.

Rose felt exhausted when they left the store. She wasn't as strong as she thought, but she had no intention of letting Mrs Luca know, because this would only lead to more unwanted fussing and pampering. She hoped they would soon be returning to the house, but her guardian turned into another enormous store.

'Here we are,' Mrs Luca said. 'Just what we need.'

Rose stared at the thousands of books and magazines that were stacked high everywhere she turned. *So many words*, she thought, *none of which would make any sense to me, even if they were written in my own language.* And there were pens and pencils and crayons in hundreds of different colours, shapes and sizes. Mrs Luca selected a variety of them before going to the checkout to pay.

'Why can't you talk, then?' Victoria asked Rose out of the blue, while they were waiting for her to return. Her question wasn't voiced unkindly. She was curious. 'Are you sure you're not pretending because you're scared?' she continued. She looked penetratingly at Rose, who blushed with discomfort. 'Just try saying "hello",' Victoria persisted.

Rose shook her head and moved closer to Mrs Luca.

'I bet I can catch you out one day,' said Victoria. 'And once I've done that we'll be able to find out a lot more about you, especially all your little secrets.'

Chapter 14

Mrs Luca scarcely left Rose alone during the next few weeks. She was determined that Rose should understand what she could and couldn't do. She enforced strict routines for mealtimes, lessons and bedtime, all of which were flouted regularly by Victoria, who only had to enlist her father's support in order to get her own way. Rose was amazed at how the girl could manipulate her father against her mother. She and Rani had been brought up to do as they were told, and Esme and Nicu formed a united front if ever there was any attempt at disobedience.

The rules of the house, and those that were specific to Rose, were many and comprehensive. Rose was convinced she would break several inadvertently. The main rules were that the kitchen, library and Mr Luca's office were out of bounds to her, as were all of the upstairs rooms apart from her bedroom. If she wanted a book to read, she must ask permission to go into the library.

'We don't want to discourage you from reading – on the contrary – but the library is Mr Luca's pride and joy. Everything is precisely catalogued, so we don't want to undo all of my husband's hard work.'

Rose was forbidden from passing time with the servants, and on no account was she to do any of the servants' work. She would be allowed to watch television for a maximum of six hours in a week and not after seven o'clock in the evening. *That's no hardship*, Rose thought to herself, *since we didn't have a television in our wagon and only ever watched it at Uncle Aleksandar's*. She would be permitted to go riding, but only accompanied by Mrs Luca or Victoria. She would be expected to maintain a respectful silence around Mr Luca's office whenever he was working from home. 'Well, that'll apply when you regain your power of speech.' Mrs Luca blushed when she realised her impropriety.

There were numerous petty rules as well. Rose was to refrain from running in the hallways and she wasn't allowed to play ball games in the gardens. At all times, she was to use the back door rather than the front, unless she was with other members of the family. At mealtimes, she would remember, please, to keep her elbows off the table, to use her napkin and to speak only when she was spoken to. Again, Mrs Luca added that she was meaning in the future, of course.

Rose was to have lessons for four hours a day, five days a week. Other than that, she was free to spend her time as she wished.

'You're still so very young,' said Mrs Luca. 'I want your childhood to be a happy one. We have so much to offer and I can see you'll thrive here.'

Finally, one of Rose's duties would be to take the dog for a walk every morning before breakfast. 'A little bit of exercise first thing will set you up well for your lessons,' Mrs Luca remarked.

Rose thought she would hate it. She wasn't keen on dogs and had taken an instant dislike to Crumble, a small, wiry dog, who seemed to yap incessantly and who kept jumping up at people. However, she discovered that once she had got into a routine, she enjoyed setting out on her own with just the dog for company. She began to form a strong bond with Crumble, who stood eagerly by the door, head cocked, ears perked up, as she changed into her boots. Once they were away from the confines of the gardens and off down the road, he scampered ahead, waited for her to catch up, scampered ahead, waited for her to catch up, until they reached the stile that led into the fields. Crumble squeezed his way under while Rose clambered over, then she picked up a stick and hurled it for him to collect. Crumble never tired of collecting sticks, or conkers, or rose hips, or the ball Rose sometimes took with her. She learnt to stop him from barking by tapping him on the nose whenever he did so, and refusing to throw anything for him to fetch until he was quiet. And he quickly learnt not to jump up at her as soon as he understood that she wouldn't be his playmate if he didn't obey.

It took Rose a while to accept that Crumble was allowed to live indoors. None of the Roma families she knew would have allowed it. But once he had earned her affection she was happy for him to sit on her feet, which he insisted upon much to Victoria's disgust, while she sat in the television room in the evening.

'You're obviously spoiling him,' Victoria said. 'He doesn't do that with anyone else, stupid animal.'

Victoria watched television a lot, Rose discovered, especially if her parents were out – and not just during the evening. She even invited Rose to watch with her one afternoon when Mr and Mrs Luca had gone into town. *But what's the point*, Rose thought, *when I can't understand what anyone's saying?*

'Come on,' Victoria persisted. 'Mummy and Daddy won't know. There's a really good film on.'

Rose hovered in the doorway, unsure what to do.

'You're such a goody-goody,' Victoria said. 'I won't tell if you don't, and you'll be bored stiff if you don't break the rules sometimes.'

Rose slowly shook her head. She didn't trust Victoria not to tell, and certainly didn't want to get into trouble when she had only been there a few weeks.

'You'll have more fun here if you make friends with me,' Victoria said another time. 'But if I take against you, I can make your life hell.'

Rose didn't doubt it, and knew that if she weren't careful Victoria would make trouble for her. The girl took delight in baiting her, then all of a sudden would transform herself into a model of amiability, acting as though she were Rose's best friend in the whole wide world.

Misconstruing this, Mrs Luca would say, 'I'm so glad you're getting on so well. I hoped you would.'

To which Victoria would reply, 'Anna will soon be like a sister to me, and I'm sure if she could speak for herself she'd say the same.' Or she would smile a fake smile, which might have fooled her mother, but not Rose.

It wasn't Victoria, though, who caused the first real

upset for Rose. It was the fact that Rose couldn't write. From the moment Mrs Luca had bought the pile of notepads and pencils, Rose knew she would be found out. She resisted Mrs Luca's initial encouragements to jot down anything she needed, but when her guardian made a very specific request that required an answer, Rose could see that either her refusal to communicate would be taken as insolence or her secret would be discovered.

Esme and Nicu could scarcely read or write, only enough to sign their names and read maps. Esme had wanted both Rose and Rani to 'have some education', and they had attended local village schools whenever they stayed in one place for long enough to make it worthwhile. However, Rose had always felt too much of a stranger among the gadje children to concentrate on lessons, and the teachers often picked on her because of her lack of what they considered to be basic skills and knowledge. She fared no better with the school-children, who sidelined her or were openly unfriendly because she was different, particularly if their parents had told them that Rose and Rani were Gypsies and not to be trusted.

Mrs Luca wanted Rose to write down her five favourite meals. 'I'll have Marina cook them for you every now and again,' she said, pleased with herself over the treat she was suggesting.

Rose looked at her blankly. Even if she had been capable of writing something down, nothing could compare to Esme's delicious meals.

'Don't be shy, Anna,' Mrs Luca persisted. 'Everyone has their favourites and I want to know yours. Here, take this pencil and notepad and make a list.'

Rose took the pencil and notepad and pretended she was thinking.

'Surely it can't be that difficult,' said Mrs Luca, beginning to sound a little impatient that her treat was being rejected. 'Write down just one meal, and we can come back to the others when you've had more time to think.'

Rose could feel herself becoming tearful. She took a deep breath and shook her head. She dared not look Mrs Luca in the face, so she stared fixedly at the floor, waiting to reap the anger that her action would undoubtedly cause.

There was no visible anger. Mrs Luca simply left the room.

Chapter 15

Rose's secret was finally uncovered by her English teacher. Mrs Conta was a short, round, bespectacled, no-nonsense sort of woman, who nevertheless had a twinkle in her eye and a big heart. She was English herself and married to a Romanian engineer, and therefore able to speak Rose's native language. When she was first introduced to Rose, she shook her hand warmly and expressed her wish that they would get on well and that, provided she studied hard, Rose would have a solid understanding of English in no time at all. Rose responded with a nod, which meant simply that she was listening, but nothing more.

'Perhaps the first words we shall hear you say will be in English.' The teacher chuckled. 'Wouldn't that surprise everyone, Anna?'

It would definitely surprise me! Rose thought.

'Don't worry,' said Mrs Conta. 'You'll be under no

pressure from me to speak if you're not ready to. There's plenty of written work we can do, and if you hear me saying the words frequently enough you'll begin to understand them and know how to use them when need be.'

She pointed to the door, a chair, a window, the clock, and said the name of each in English. She wrote the words on a whiteboard and asked Rose to copy them into a notepad. Rose didn't even pick up a pencil. She sat in her chair with her eyes lowered.

'Copy what I've written, please, Anna,' Mrs Conta instructed.

When she saw that Rose was making no attempt to do as she was told, the teacher sat down next to her.

'What's going on here, then?' she said. 'Do I have a disobedient child in front of me? Do I have a child who doesn't want to learn? Do I have a child who is too unhappy to be bothered? Or do I have a child who, quite simply, can't write?' She watched Rose carefully. 'Look at me, Anna,' she said gently.

When she said it for a second time, Rose looked at her.

'Why are you crying?' Mrs Conta asked. 'A child who's being disobedient doesn't cry. A child who doesn't want to learn doesn't cry. But a child who is unhappy, or a child who's frightened to admit that she can't do what she's being asked to do might cry. Which is it, Anna, or is it both things?'

She took Rose's hand. 'Squeeze my hand once if you're unhappy, twice if the writing is the problem, or three times if it's both.'

Rose squeezed the teacher's hand once, paused, squeezed again, almost imperceptibly, then hesitated, before pulling her hand away.

'If that's the problem, then it's a problem we can do something about. I will teach you how to write,' Mrs Conta said brightly. 'And I won't tell, if that's what you're worried about, though I can't guarantee your secret won't be found out.'

Rose was so grateful, but she was anxious as well. Writing had always seemed such a strange thing to do and she wasn't sure she could master it, especially since a lot of her Roma friends and family were unable to write. *What if not being able to write is in my blood?*

She picked up the pencil and held it in her hand the way she had been shown in the past and the way Mrs Conta was demonstrating now. For the next half an hour, she copied shapes and lines until she could keep the pencil from wobbling and had stopped gouging deep furrows into the paper. Occasionally, she wanted to hurl the pencil across the room, frustrated at the constant repetition and at being confined indoors for so long, but when she had mastered the letters *r*, *o*, *s* and *e* and carefully consigned them to her memory, she was happy with her achievement. *I'll always be Rose if I can write my name.*

'You're lucky your name has only two different letters in it,' Mrs Conta had said at the beginning of the lesson. 'You'll master it in no time.'

It was true. Rose was soon able to write *anna*, though she had no more emotional attachment to the word than to *luca*.

She liked Mrs Conta. The teacher was kind without being treacly, firm without being harsh. She seemed to understand Rose's needs. She didn't probe, but responded sympathetically whenever Rose appeared distant or sad. She didn't ask Rose to write down what she was feeling, even when she was proficient enough to be able to express herself on the page.

Rose began to look forward to her lessons. The whole process of sitting still, listening and learning was alien to her, and she had to get used to being closeted in a room for hours on end, but she found herself becoming hungry to learn more. She especially enjoyed discovering about England's history. When she heard there was a queen who lived in a huge palace, she wanted to go and see her.

'Is she beautiful?' she wrote using words and pictures.

'She has a kind face and she works very hard for her people,' said the teacher. 'Perhaps one day Mrs Luca might take you to London to see the palace, but very few people meet the queen.'

Rose had visions of looking up and catching a glimpse of the queen framed by one of the palace windows. She would wave to her and tell her that she was unhappy in her country and would like, if you please, to go home.

Mrs Conta brought her magazines with photographs of famous places in England, like Trafalgar Square with its lion statues, Stonehenge with its huge prehistoric stones, the white cliffs of Dover overlooking the sea, Windsor Castle, where the queen sometimes lived, as well as Buckingham Palace itself. Rose gazed at them in awe – they were all on such an enormous scale compared to anything she had come across in her previous life.

She felt more at home when Mrs Conta showed her pictures of country villages with narrow, winding lanes and cottages decked with flowers. She could imagine being with her parents and brother in their wagon, trotting slowly along the lanes, Nicu with his pipe in his mouth, Esme humming quietly with her sewing on her lap and Rani chattering non-stop. Some of the villages were so pretty! *If only I might be allowed to walk around them one day*, Rose brooded.

'Perhaps Mrs Luca will be happy for me to take you out for the day,' Mrs Conta suggested when she saw Rose pass her fingers wistfully over the photograph of a river lined with bulrushes and overhung with willows. 'Would you like that?'

Rose nodded quickly, her eyes lighting up.

'I'll see what I can do, but first it's time for maths.'

Rose pulled a face. She loathed maths and felt hopeless at it. As long as she could count she didn't see the need for complicated calculations, however hard Mrs Conta tried to make her understand their usefulness.

'Sour faces won't get you anywhere,' Mrs Conta responded to her pouts, 'whereas knowing your multiplication tables will come in very handy in lots of different situations.'

Rose pulled another long face, which made Mrs Conta laugh, but tried to concentrate on the numbers the teacher was writing on the board.

From time to time, Mrs Luca would pop her head round the door to see how they were getting on. Mrs Conta would always praise Rose's efforts.

'Anna is a model pupil,' she said. 'She's very curious and picks things up quickly.'

'Good,' said Mrs Luca. 'I'm delighted to hear that we'll soon be able to communicate with her properly.'

Chapter 16

When lessons were over and at weekends, Rose was allowed to wander freely around the grounds of the house. She couldn't wait! She let herself out of the back door and took deep breaths of the fresh air that welcomed her. Summer was almost over. The leaves on the trees were turning crisp and golden, prey to sudden gusts of wind that would break their fragile hold and send them twirling downward in a last dance of life.

Rose loved the autumn. Back home, her family used to ramble through woods and meadows in search of edible mushrooms to sell in nearby villages. They would travel the country looking for work helping farmers to harvest their crops. It was always a race to be there first, ahead of other Roma families. There was only so much work to go round. Nicu prided himself on the relationship he had built over the years with farmers who were happy to employ him because they knew he could be trusted. He and the family would set up camp on a farmer's land and dig for potatoes or pick peas and beans. Rose preferred the peas and beans. It was back-breaking work sifting the earth for potatoes.

Rose was growing used to life at the Lucas' house and could even appreciate some aspects of it. She enjoyed spending time in the garden, wandering from one area to another. She played on an old tyre swing and climbing frame that used to belong to Victoria, which Mrs Luca had asked Goran to set up for her. She liked to sit on the edge of the pond and watch the fish, running her fingers gently through the water and trying to spot snails on the water lily leaves. *Fifteen today*, she would count to herself. *Twenty-eight today!*

If she had to be cooped up anywhere, Rose could think of worse places than her bedroom. She wouldn't have dreamt of swapping it for her tiny bed in the wagon and the closeness of her family, but she had never before experienced such comfort and it was the perfect place for her to take refuge and just be herself.

Rose looked forward more and more to her lessons with Mrs Conta. She had never thought she would enjoy learning in a classroom environment, but Mrs Conta made it fun. *She's so nice*, Rose thought. *Some gadje are nice. I wish Esme and Nicu could have met her. They would've liked her and been happy for me to spend time with her.*

Rose would sometimes come across Goran as she walked through the gardens. When he wasn't driving a lawnmower up and down the extensive lawns, much of his time was spent clearing leaves from the paths and plucking them out of the pond. He always touched his cap to her, but his manner was less than respectful.

'Not a bad place to wind up, is it?' He smirked. 'You could've done worse for yourself.'

Rose didn't know how to respond. She nodded blankly.

'Cat got your tongue, has it? Bet I could find it for you. Mind you, I think I'd let the cat have my tongue if it meant I could move into a place like this.'

Everything he said was delivered with the same big smile, his lips wrapped round a mouth full of overlarge teeth, two of which were capped with gold.

'She's a bit of a soft touch is the mistress of the house, as well as being rather beautiful. Don't you go upsetting her, will you? I reckon it wouldn't take much to turn her from a pussy cat into a tiger.'

Rose was shocked that he should discuss Mrs Luca in such a way, and decided to avoid him in case he tried to share more of his opinions about Mrs Luca. It wasn't easy. He often appeared as if from nowhere when she stopped to look at the fish, or to smell a flower, or simply to enjoy being outside.

'They're worth a lot of money, those fish,' he said, catching Rose off guard as she held out a finger for one of them to suck to see what it would feel like. 'He's obsessed with them, Mr Luca is. He'd go potty if anything happened to them.'

Rose pulled her finger back quickly as though she'd been bitten, which caused Goran to laugh out loud.

'Unless you've put a curse on him, I don't think that's going to do any harm,' he chuckled, 'which is a shame, because personally I can't stand the ugly brutes.'

Rose attempted to walk away, but he caught her arm. 'Rumour has it you're a Gypsy.' He searched her face. 'Nothing wrong with that, though, is there? As long as things don't start to go missing.' He laughed out loud again. 'Off you go, miss.'

Rose was relieved when he wasn't around, and knew she was safe if his truck wasn't parked behind the sheds. She took to checking first before going into the walled gardens, where there was no escaping him. Alternatively, she set off in the opposite direction to reach the stables. She loved wandering up and down here, stroking the horses and feeding them with the sugar lumps Marina gave her when nobody was looking. If the stable boy was there she nodded at him shyly, but otherwise ignored him. He largely ignored her too, though she sometimes caught him staring at her.

Mrs Luca had charged Victoria with helping Rose choose which of the two ponies would be hers. Victoria had saddled each of them up in turn and tutted while Rose struggled to mount.

'Mummy said you knew how to ride,' she said impatiently.

'*Yes, I know how to ride,*' Rose wanted to shout with frustration. '*I know how to ride with my body next to the horse's body so that he can feel and understand what I want him to do and I can feel him too.*'

She detested the oversized riding hat that Mrs Luca forced her to wear, and thought she would die of embarrassment when Victoria led her round the yard with the pony on a lead, especially when Mrs Luca arrived and clapped her hands.

'Well done, Anna,' she said. 'You look quite at home up there. Now, which pony are you going to choose?'

Rose pointed reluctantly to the piebald, though she had no desire to ride either of them.

'That's a good choice,' Mrs Luca agreed. 'Kosta's very placid and easy to handle. Well, now, I'm pleased. We're making such good progress. As soon as you're confident, Anna, we'll all go for a ride together.'

Rose saw Victoria pull a face and fought against doing the same thing.

When, a few days later and first thing in the morning, they set off along the lane, Victoria leading, Rose in the middle, Mrs Luca behind and Crumble scampering along the verge, Rose's only enjoyment was breathing in the morning air and listening to the birdsong. Dressed in newly purchased jodhpurs, riding jacket and hat, she felt as though she had been squeezed into clothing designed for someone half her size. Victoria and Mrs Luca were wearing similar outfits, and Rose wondered if they were as uncomfortable as she was. Victoria sat unnaturally straight-backed, Rose thought, and seemed not to be interested in the early morning sights and sounds.

Mrs Luca kept checking that Rose was managing all right and not tiring herself out too much.

'It's so easy to forget that you spent nearly three months in hospital not so many weeks ago,' she said. 'You look so much healthier now.'

'She's fine, Mummy. Stop fussing over her,' Victoria said without turning her head.

It's true, Rose admitted to herself. She had filled out all round and her hair was thick and shiny, though Mrs Luca had insisted on having it cut shorter, 'to make you look more modern and less like . . . less unkempt'. She wanted to laugh, however, at the suggestion that she might tire herself out sitting on a horse and doing nothing more strenuous than trotting up a lane. She hoped they might break into a canter at least, but soon they took a short cut along a bridleway and arrived back at the house.

'Did you enjoy that, Anna?' Mrs Luca asked as they dismounted.

Rose nodded her head and tried to look grateful.

Victoria snorted. 'It's not going to be the most exciting thing she's ever done in her life, is it, Mummy? Leave her alone, poor girl.'

For a moment Rose thought Victoria was being sympathetic towards her, but she quickly realised that the girl was simply having another dig at Mrs Luca. It saddened her to witness the awkwardness of their relationship, especially when she compared it to the warmth of her own with Esme. Victoria seemed to delight in being at loggerheads with her mother, whereas Rose had hated the times when she and Esme had had cross words. She hoped Esme had known how much she loved her, but doubted that Mrs Luca could ever feel certain of her daughter's love. As they walked back through the gardens, Rose resolved to make every effort to be good and helpful to her guardian, who must at times find it hard to bring a real smile to her face.

Chapter 17

One of Mr Luca's koi carp died. It was the one Rose had allowed to suck her finger.

Mr Luca raged through the house after he discovered it lying belly up in the pond. 'I've had that fish since the time we put in the pond. It was worth a fortune. There was no reason for it to die. None whatsoever.'

'It must have been ill,' said Mrs Luca. 'You wouldn't have been able to tell.'

'Of course I'd have been able to tell. I looked at them all yesterday. I look at them all every day. They were all perfectly healthy. I wouldn't put it past that Goran to have dropped something in the water. I've never trusted the man, but you would have your way over him.'

'Don't be so silly, darling,' Mrs Luca remonstrated. 'Goran's been with us for four years now and his behaviour has always been exemplary.'

'A worm can turn,' Mr Luca growled. 'It's a conspiracy, that's what it is. Just when things are already going wrong, they get worse.'

However hard Mrs Luca tried, her husband was not to be pacified. Rose withdrew to her room. She knew she had done nothing wrong, but was terrified Goran might suggest that she had put a curse on the fish. She had no choice but to obey when she was called down to dinner, and she entered the dining room full of fear that the spotlight would fall on her.

The tension in the air was palpable. Even Victoria was subdued in the face of her father's anger. Mr Luca complained about everything. The meal was too cold, the meat was tough, Mrs Luca was spending too much money.

He turned his attention to Rose. 'What have you got to say for yourself, then?' he demanded.

Rose gazed down at her plate.

'Well?' Mr Luca persisted. 'I'm spending all this money on you and you're still maintaining this stubborn silence.'

'Don't,' Mrs Luca protested.

'Don't what?'

'Don't be so heartless.'

'Heartless! I'm providing this child with a home and

everything that goes with it, and you're calling me heartless! Foolish, more like. As for all the other waifs and strays you've netted, it's a wonder I'm not completely penniless already.'

'Can we have this conversation in private rather than in front of the girls?' Mrs Luca said in a low voice.

'It'll do Anna, or whatever her name is, good to understand the sacrifices we're making. Perhaps then she'll make a little more effort.'

'I don't know how you dare talk about *our* sacrifices in front of her,' Mrs Luca hissed.

'I dare because this is my house, and I'll do what I like in it!' Mr Luca pushed back his chair and stormed out of the room, passing Marina on the way and rebuking her for another poor meal.

'Please don't worry. You do very well, Marina,' Mrs Luca assured her as she cleared the dishes. 'My husband is a little upset, that's all.'

'Over the death of a fish!' Victoria smirked. 'Daddy never could control his anger.'

'You don't understand what he's going through, and you know very well how important those fish are to your father,' Mrs Luca chided.

'He doesn't need to take it out on everyone else,

though, does he?' said Victoria. 'Poor Anna must be shaking in her shoes.'

Rose looked in surprise at Victoria.

'Mind you, he does have a point,' Victoria continued, holding Rose's stare.

'What do you mean?' her mother asked.

'Doesn't matter,' said Victoria. 'Let's just hope he doesn't find any more dead fish. Hey, Mummy, do you think that's what "carpe diem" really means, and not "seize the day"? Do you get it? "The carp died." You have to think of it written down.'

'That's a dreadful joke,' said Mrs Luca, 'but I'm glad some Latin is sinking in.'

'Latin's a waste of time and money,' Victoria said, pouting.

'Not if you're going to be a doctor,' Mrs Luca argued.

'*You* want me to be a doctor. I don't want to be a doctor.'

'Your father and I both want you to be a doctor. It's a fine profession. It's what I would have chosen for myself if I'd had the opportunity.'

'Instead, you married a rich businessman and you don't ever have to work. What about Anna? What do you want Anna to be?'

Rose frowned as she became the centre of attention again.

'Anna's much younger than you,' said Mrs Luca. 'It's far too early for us to worry about that yet.'

'You don't know how old she is. Ask her to write down her age.'

Rose quickly held up ten fingers.

'When's your birthday, then?' Victoria demanded.

Luckily, there was no paper immediately to hand, since Rose didn't know her exact date of birth, only the month, and she didn't want Victoria watching her struggle to write it down. But in any case, Mrs Luca, who had looked increasingly uncomfortable during her daughter's interrogation, suddenly interrupted her.

'Anna's birthday is just as it says on the papers we had drawn up for her, since there were none of her own to be found. November the twentieth.'

'That's sick,' said Victoria. 'That's really sick.'

'Quiet!' Mrs Luca turned on her angrily. 'You weren't asked for your opinion.'

Rose was astounded to learn she had a new birth month. Her real birthday was in February, though Esme and Nicu hadn't always celebrated it on the same date every year. 'It's around the fourth,' Esme had told her, 'but we've got a bit confused. It doesn't really make much difference.'

Rose had had her tenth birthday in February, and now

she was going to have her eleventh birthday less than ten months later. She realised she was losing her entire identity. She was becoming someone else – 'Anna' was taking over.

'For your birthday, Anna,' Mrs Luca was saying, 'I thought we'd go to a theme park.'

'What? You've never taken *me* to a theme park!' Victoria was outraged.

'I know, darling,' said Mrs Luca. 'It'll be a treat for both of you. You'd like that, wouldn't you, Anna?'

Rose didn't know what a theme park was. She nodded, because it sounded as though it was something she should be very happy about, but she was still coming to terms with the idea of having a new birthday and turning eleven sooner than she had expected.

'I certainly shan't be going on any rides myself.' Mrs Luca pulled a face. 'So the two of you will be able to go off together.'

Rose wondered if Mrs Luca was unwell when she said she wouldn't be going on any rides. She was appalled at the thought of going off with Victoria on her own, trotting obediently along on Kosta while Victoria galloped into the distance on Griffin.

'Oh, whoopee-doo,' Victoria snorted. 'If Anna keeps

up her vow of silence she won't even be able to have a good scream.'

'I'm sure you'll make up for it, darling,' said Mrs Luca. 'And it'll be a good chance for me to get some photos of you together.'

The conversation had ceased to make any sense to Rose. She hadn't a clue what they were talking about and why she should want to scream, but it made her very anxious.

Mrs Luca stood up from the table. 'Goodnight, Anna dear. You're looking tired. Take yourself off to bed now, and have sweet dreams.'

Chapter 18

When Rose wasn't having lessons, Mrs Luca involved her in everything from shopping for food to browsing garden centres to going to church, where the congregation looked at her curiously, wondering perhaps where she had suddenly appeared from. Rose noticed that Mrs Luca kept herself very much to herself, answering politely if spoken to, but not encouraging conversation. Victoria absented herself whenever she could, disappearing off to meet friends, taking one of the horses out, or claiming to be tired. Her mother tried hard to knit them together as a family, but neither Victoria nor her father made much effort, and Rose herself was happier to rub along with Mrs Luca on her own, rather than cope with the multifarious tensions that arose when they were all together.

The extravagant spending sprees that Mrs Luca

indulged in were in stark contrast to daily life inside the Lucas' home, which Rose found to be cheerless, apart from lesson-time. Rose missed the noise, the colour and the variety of life with her family and their Roma friends. One of the things she missed most was music. Music had been such a big part of her life with Esme and Nicu. From the age of four, she had accompanied her parents and members of their extended family on the tambourine – not always in time, but with great gusto. She had pressed the keys and buttons on Esme's accordion and watched in awe as her mother pushed the bellows in and out. She had first picked up the bow to her father's violin when she was just two, and scraped it across the strings while he held the instrument still and moved his fingers on the fret. It had amused him to watch her, but as she grew older and he realised that she had a good ear and a natural sense of rhythm, he encouraged her to play whenever she showed the slightest bit of interest.

Victoria listened to pop music in her bedroom behind her closed door, but nothing was left of it apart from the boom and thud of bass and drum by the time it filtered through the thick walls. Once in a while Mrs Luca turned on the radio to listen to a play, and Mr Luca never missed the news, but they rarely switched over to music.

One day, Rose was left alone in the house while Mr Luca was at a meeting and Mrs Luca took Victoria out for the afternoon.

'We're going to spend some mother and daughter time together,' Mrs Luca explained to Rose. 'I'm sure you understand, don't you, Anna? Marina will be here till late, and Goran is outside, so you'll be perfectly safe.'

Rose nodded, delighted. She watched them slide into a car and waved as they departed down the drive. *Thank goodness!* she thought. She grabbed a handful of gravel and threw it up in the air. She wanted to run through the gardens and dabble her hands in the pond. She wanted to free one of the horses and gallop away across the fields.

'Don't go doing anything naughty while they're away, will you, miss?'

Rose spun round and came face to face with Goran. He grinned at her slyly.

'Here, I've got some chocolate. Do you want some?'

Rose shook her head and turned to go back into the house.

'Too hoity-toity to accept a bit of chocolate from a gardener, are we?' Goran sneered. 'A few posh clothes don't change who you are, miss. I'll be keeping an eye on you.'

Rose fled indoors. Her delight at being left on her own was banished in that one brief moment. She would have to stay inside for the remainder of the afternoon. She wouldn't dare to go back out and risk more abuse.

The house was so silent. Wherever Marina was, she wasn't making any noise. Rose wanted to know her whereabouts, just in case she needed her. Much as she had longed to be left alone, Rose felt daunted by the size and sombreness of the Lucas' home. She tiptoed along the hallway, not because she was scared of being discovered, but because it seemed wrong to break the silence. The mere fact of being alone, though, made her anxious that someone or something might be lurking in the shadows and jump out at her. When Rose reached the kitchen and found the door was ajar, she stood and listened, then, heart in mouth, pushed the door gently until it was open wide enough for her to see inside.

The kitchen was huge – even bigger than it had looked from the outside when she had peeped through the windows – and empty. The walls were lined with cupboards above and below, work surfaces that stretched right the way round, and all manner of appliances. In the middle was an enormous square island, with yet more cupboards topped by a thick slab of polished wood.

A strong ironwork frame was suspended above it, from which numerous cooking utensils were hanging. Rose couldn't understand why anyone would need so many different pots and pans, especially a family as small as the Luca family. She hovered in the doorway, undecided as to what to do next.

Something was cooking. Drawn by the rather delicious smell, Rose ventured across the tiled floor and peered through the glass front of one of the ovens. A large tart was browning, sugar bubbling stickily between neatly cut slices of apples and pears.

Esme used to make apple dumplings, Rose remembered. As a family, they had gone apple-picking for orchard owners and were allowed to keep some of the spoils. Nicu would climb a ladder and delve among the branches of a tree to wrest ripe fruits from their stalks, before dropping them for Rose to catch. Rani would try to catch them too, but he was butterfingered and they would fall through his hands or, worse, hit him on the head, though that didn't stop him coming back for more. Esme would set Rani to work looking under trees for apples that had already fallen and were perfect in every way, while she searched for damaged fruit that could always be turned into apple jelly or jam or pickle.

Rose had loved helping Esme to cook. Sometimes

they spent hours at their little stove, or in front of a log fire at the edge of a wood, using recipes that had been passed down through generations. It made her feel as though she was becoming part of her family history just by keeping such practices going, and she knew that when she had children herself she would pass on the same recipes to them.

The memories and the smell of the baking tart made Rose feel hungry. An open packet of biscuits was lying on the central island. She walked over slowly and picked it up. *Surely nobody will notice if I have just one biscuit?* she thought to herself. *And if they do, surely they won't mind?*

Rose was about to take one when there was a loud knock on the window. She dropped the packet in fright, then stared in horror as several biscuits spilled out across the floor, broken. She looked up to see Goran outside, wagging his finger at her and leering. She fled from the kitchen and ran upstairs to her bedroom, where she threw herself on to the bed and burst into tears.

Rose lay there weeping over Goran's behaviour towards her, then for everything she had lost and in fear for her future. When she could weep no more, she dreamed of running away and somehow finding her way home to her own country and to her remaining family and friends. It didn't matter how kind Mrs Luca tried to be, Rose couldn't help feeling that something rotten lay at the core of her carefully manicured world. Something rotten that threatened Rose herself. More immediately, it was Goran who threatened her, yet she had done nothing to incite his sinister interest in her. She dared not go downstairs now and she despaired at the sense that she was being confined to an ever smaller place on the Lucas' vast estate.

From somewhere deep inside, though, Rose discovered a nugget of defiance. *I can't go outside and I can't go downstairs, but I refuse to be cooped up in this room*, she thought angrily.

She slid off the bed and headed for the door, opening it quietly and stepping out on to the landing. The hooded eyes of someone's ancestor stared at her disapprovingly from a gloomy portrait on the wall opposite. Rose stuck her tongue out at him and giggled inwardly. She had made up her mind to explore, and no miserable old bore was going to stop her. As she slipped along the landing, she felt excited and anxious, but above all she felt more alive than at any time since the accident. She was doing what she wanted – instead of what she was told – and that made her heart beat strongly.

Rose arrived at Victoria's room. The door was firmly shut, as it always was, with a notice attached to the handle warning of the dire consequences to be suffered by anyone who entered. It was a challenge Rose couldn't resist. She strained her ears to check that there were no sounds from anywhere close by, then, heart racing, she swiftly took hold of the handle, turned it and pushed the door back.

She was shocked by what she found. The room was beautiful – or should have been. The walls were lined with a pale pink paper that looked like silk. Thick, raspberry-coloured velvet curtains hung ornately around the windows. The carpet was richly patterned in pinks and greens and yellows. The bed, big enough for six people, like her own, had a canopy of cream organza drapes. But the room was a shambles. Every single drawer of the chest of drawers was half open and spilling out clothes. The dressing table was piled high with pots of cream with their lids off, several combs and brushes sprouting weeks' worth of hair, pieces of jewellery and scarves, piles of CDs with no cases and endless screwed-up tissues. More tissues surrounded the base of a bin, which was full to the brim. Discarded items of clothing and oddments of underwear covered the floor, and shoes were scattered everywhere, none of them in pairs. The doors of the wardrobe, which extended the full length of one wall, were open wide enough to reveal a similar chaos behind them.

I can't believe Mrs Luca allows her daughter to live like this, Rose reflected. Esme wouldn't have allowed it. There wasn't room in the wagon for any of the family to be untidy, and it was important to her that they were immaculate at the beginning and end of the day, whatever might transpire in between. Whether they worked in muddy fields, travelled for miles on dusty roads, or gorged themselves on blackberries and other messy fruits, when the day was over Esme would dispatch Rose and Nicu to fetch buckets of water from a nearby river or village tap. She inspected Rose and Rani while they washed, and wielded the sponge herself if they weren't doing the job properly. Even Nicu caught the wrath of her sponge if he tried to skimp on his ablutions.

Rose picked up a tube of lipstick from the dressing table. It was gold with a tiny red crystal embedded in one side. She loved the smoothness of the metal and toyed with the crystal, pressing her finger against it and studying the indentation on her skin. She removed the top from the tube. The lipstick was ice pink. She held it up to her mouth. *Do I dare?* Esme always wore bright red, she recalled – the colour of roses, her favourite flower. Rose wondered what pink would look like against her dark Romani skin. *There's only one way to*

119

find out. If Victoria knew she'd go berserk! She tightened her lips and painted them, first the upper then the lower, and stared at herself in the mirror. She pulled a face. The pink didn't suit her at all. There was a box of tissues by the side of the bed. She grabbed one quickly and rubbed her lips hard, upset that she had allowed herself to use something as intimate as a gadje's lipstick.

Rose shut the bedroom door tight on the wreckage and moved on to the next one. She was disappointed to discover that it hid nothing more than shelf upon shelf of bedding and towels, all neatly arranged by size and colour. A muffled clattering of pans from downstairs made her hesitate briefly before continuing. She was glad to know that Marina was around, but felt safe to carry on.

She crossed to the other side of the landing and peered into a vast bathroom that boasted an armchair and thick white rugs. Rose wondered whom it was for, since she assumed that Mr and Mrs Luca had their own private bathroom within their bedroom, and so far no visitors had stayed at the house. There was another bedroom adjacent to it, beautifully furnished and with the bed made up, but clearly not used. It had a musty smell about it, which made Rose wrinkle up her nose and withdraw quickly.

At the very end of the landing was one final room to be explored. First, though, Rose went back along the landing to the top of the stairs and listened. She was surprised to hear the sound of music and singing. She smiled to herself when she realised that Marina was making the most of her employers' absence by singing her head off to tunes on the radio. Satisfied that the housekeeper was happily occupied, Rose made for the final door and opened it tentatively.

Chapter 19

The room was in darkness. Rose sneezed as soon as she entered and tried to make out the shapes that were just visible in the gloom. She thought there was a bed, but wasn't sure because it seemed too high. She ran her hand over the wall to find the light switch, but when she found it and flipped it, nothing happened. There was something forbidding about this room that made Rose want to close the door and flee, yet curiosity made her determined to stay her ground. She felt her way to the windows, where thick velvet curtains blocked out all trace of the day. She hesitated, then pulled at one of the curtains.

A ray of sunshine fell on a grand piano that dominated the centre of the room. Myriad particles of dust hovered in the sunlight, released suddenly from their resting place and unwilling to settle again. Rose pulled the curtain back further. More light flooded in. The room seemed to devour it, like an animal that has been deprived of food and suddenly has a bowlful put in front of it. A musical score lay open on the top of the piano, though the lid of the piano was closed. Rose crossed the room and trailed her finger over the lid. It was thick with dust.

She could see enough now to identify other objects in the room. A wide, glass-fronted cupboard was filled with musical scores and biographies of famous composers, though to Rose they were just rather dull-looking books. A music stand stood in the corner. On the floor next to it, leaning up against the wall, was a violin. Rose's heart skipped a beat at the sight of it. She bent down and stroked its smooth wooden body. She picked it up, blew the dust off it and plucked one of the strings. The noise was both familiar and foreign. Rose searched the room for the bow, and found it by the side of the cupboard. She laid it across the strings of the violin, drew it back gently, carefully, and tittered at the thin, squeaky sound that quivered in the air with the dust.

'You'll have to do better than that,' she mouthed.

Memories of music her father had taught her overwhelmed Rose as she fiddled with the keys to tune the violin. She wanted to hear them again, *feel* them again, not just in her head, but through her entire body. She had been starved of them for so long! She now understood how much music had been in her father's soul, and that she was ready for that feeling to invade her own soul. She plucked the strings one by one, before drawing the bow across them again. This time the sound was fuller, rounder, more melodic. Rose adjusted the keys one last time, lifted the violin to her shoulder and began to play.

She was rusty at first – so rusty that she nearly hurled the instrument away in frustration – but gradually her bowing became smoother and the sound she produced began to please her. Rose closed her eyes and allowed the music to wash through her. It gave her a sense of well-being. It made her happy. It made her believe she would be free again to listen to the comforting *clip-clop* of a horse's hooves on the narrow lanes of her homeland.

When she opened her eyes again, Marina was standing before her.

'You play well,' the housekeeper said.

Alarmed at what she might do next, Rose lowered the violin to her side.

'But the mistress would not be happy to find you here.'

Rose shook her head and shuffled towards the door, hoping Marina would note the pleading look on her face.

'I won't tell,' Marina assured her, closing the curtains. 'What use is a violin if nobody plays it?'

Rose nodded and hurried out of the room. Marina followed and closed the door behind her.

'Beware of upsetting the mistress,' she warned Rose. 'And if you want a biscuit, you know I'll let you have one.'

Chapter 20

It was raining on the morning of Rose's new birthday. Rose didn't mind. She jumped out of bed early to take Crumble for his walk and didn't stop to put on a raincoat. They headed for the woods that lined the fields. By the time they reached them she was already soaked.

It was dry under the canopy of trees. Rose kicked her way through the fallen leaves and laughed as Crumble pounced on them barking excitedly. She was rather looking forward to the day now that she had got used to the idea of a second birthday. Mrs Luca had shown her a leaflet about the theme park and she understood from the photographs what had been meant by 'rides'. She had been to a fairground with Esme and Nicu once and some of their friends worked in fairgrounds, but those were small affairs compared to this theme park.

'I bet you'll be terrified,' Victoria had said to her. 'You don't look like someone who'll enjoy being turned upside down high up in the air. You'll probably be sick.'

No, I won't, Rose thought. *I'm not as pathetic as you think.*

They had been sitting in front of the television the previous evening. Victoria seemed determined to spoil Rose's birthday treat even before it had begun. Rose stared fixedly at the screen, trying not to react. She knew enough English now to be able to follow some of what was happening.

'Of course, Mummy's only planned this to make herself feel better. It won't work, though. Nothing ever does.' She paused before continuing. 'Do you think that if you're absolutely petrified, you'll scream and then your voice will come back?'

Rose shrugged – she had no idea herself. If it did, she would be as surprised as anyone.

'If I couldn't speak, I'd want someone to take me out and shoot me, because I'd be so frustrated at not being able to tell people what I was thinking and feeling,' Victoria said. 'Especially if I couldn't read or write, either.'

Rose made to stand up.

'I don't think you can read or write, can you? You

certainly couldn't when you arrived here. I had a sneaky look through the door after one of your lessons and I could tell from what was written on the board. I can't imagine why Mrs Conta hasn't said anything. Mummy hasn't worked it out yet, or if she has she hasn't mentioned it, but that's probably because she doesn't want to admit that her protégée is so . . . backward. Daddy would have a fit if he knew he was paying good money just for you to learn the alphabet.'

Rose moved to the door.

'Don't worry, though, Anna. It can be our big secret, can't it?'

Rose fled to her bedroom. She still couldn't understand why Victoria was always so obnoxious to her, though she could appreciate that it must be difficult suddenly having to share her life with a new 'sister'. '*I didn't ask to be here, either,*' Rose wanted to tell her. '*If I had a choice, I'd be back home with my family in Romania.*' The older girl seemed to go out of her way to goad her, yet Rose did nothing to encourage it. It made Rose more determined not to allow Victoria to ruin the few opportunities that came her way to enjoy herself. Tomorrow was her treat and she was going to make the most of it, even if she wasn't sure how she would react to being turned upside down high up in the air.

Now, as she walked back towards the house, Crumble scampering at her heels, Rose remembered what Victoria had said about nothing ever making Mrs Luca feel better. *What does that mean? What's wrong with Mrs Luca?* she wondered. There were so many things about this family that perplexed her. Perhaps this was always the way with gadje families.

Rose pushed it out of her mind, went through the back door of the house, dried Crumble's feet and poured some biscuits into his bowl. She was about to go from the utility room into the hall, when Mrs Luca appeared.

'Ah, there you are, Anna. Goodness me, child, you're soaked through. Why didn't you put on a coat?'

She didn't wait for a reply, but continued, 'I'm afraid it's bad news. Victoria has an upset tummy, so we won't be able to go to the theme park today. I can't possibly abandon her when she's feeling so unwell. You do understand, don't you? And judging by the weather, it wouldn't have been ideal anyway. But we'll celebrate your birthday here and I know you'll love the present we've got you.'

Her words came out unnaturally fast and Rose could tell that Mrs Luca was as disappointed as she was.

'Victoria is very sorry to have spoilt your treat, of course, and I know she was looking forward to it too.

I'm sure we can rearrange it for another day. Now, go and get some dry clothes on and then come and see what we've bought you. And if the weather clears, perhaps you and I could take the horses out later.'

Rose trudged upstairs. It was never going to be a perfect day, but anything would have been better than staying in the house and trying to look as though she was enjoying herself. She might have guessed Victoria would find a way to ruin things for her. She wanted to lock herself in her bedroom and stay there until the next morning. She didn't want this birthday. It wasn't real, and now it would be worse than a normal day. Reluctantly, she dried her hair and changed her clothes. She took as long as she could, until she heard Mrs Luca calling her and braved herself to go back downstairs.

Mr and Mrs Luca were waiting for her in the dining room. Mr Luca wished her a happy birthday over the top of his newspaper. Mrs Luca ushered her to a chair at the top of the table and called for Marina, who appeared with a mountainous breakfast of cold meats and cheeses and fruit and pastries.

'Tuck in, Anna,' said Mrs Luca. 'And a very happy birthday to you – the first of many with us.'

Rose attempted a smile, but felt so awkward that

her appetite deserted her. Mrs Luca urged her to take more than she wanted, and encouraged her to clear her plate.

'Go on, enjoy every last mouthful,' she said. 'I want this to be a very special day!'

Mr Luca raised his eyebrows and tutted, but Mrs Luca ignored him.

'As soon as you've finished, you can open your present. I'm so excited for you to see it.'

Rose forced down the last piece of cheese and wiped her hands on her napkin.

'I do so wish I knew what you were thinking,' Mrs Luca sighed. 'I suppose it's too much to expect you to carry a notepad around with you.'

'She's probably wishing you'd stop clucking over her,' Mr Luca observed. 'Can't we just get this present thing out of the way so that I can get on with my work?'

'Close your eyes, then, Anna,' said Mrs Luca.

Rose did as she was told, though it made her feel vulnerable. She heard a cupboard door being opened and closed and a rustling of paper.

'You can open them again.'

Mrs Luca was standing behind a huge rectangular parcel wrapped in gaily coloured paper. Half a dozen smaller parcels were on the side table next to her.

'Happy birthday again, Anna. We hope you'll have hours of fun playing with this.'

Rose stood rooted to the spot, not daring to move forward and take possession of the proffered gifts.

'Well, if you don't want it, we'll give it to somebody else,' Mr Luca blustered.

'Shhh, darling. Come, Anna, I'll help you unwrap it.' Mrs Luca beckoned her closer and pointed to the top corner of the large parcel.

Rose took hold of the paper and began to undo it very carefully.

'Give it a jolly good pull,' Mrs Luca urged.

Rose stared at her as though she were mad – Esme would have been appalled at such waste – then tore into the paper, now eager herself to discover what it concealed. What looked like a roof appeared first, followed by a wall with windows and a door. Rose stepped back, puzzled.

'Do you see what it is, Anna?' asked Mrs Luca.

Rose shook her head.

'It's the front wall of a doll's house – your doll's house. Look, behind it are three more outside walls.'

Mrs Luca pulled the first wall aside to reveal one of the side walls. She pulled that aside to reveal a further wall inset with a back door and another side wall.

'Do you see it now?' she asked, her voice full of excitement.

Rose nodded, though she had no idea what she was supposed to do with it. She tried to look pleased.

'Well, that went down like a lead balloon, didn't it?' muttered Mr Luca. 'Can I go now?' He headed for the door. 'Enjoy your day,' he aimed at Rose and managed a smile.

'Open the other boxes, Anna.' Mrs Luca pressed on, anxious for her excitement to be shared.

Rose opened one box after another. There were more walls – smaller ones – and flooring and doors. There were beds and cupboards, chairs and tables, appliances for the kitchen, baths and showers, all of them needing to be assembled. One box contained grass and plants and paving; another was filled with people; yet another contained animals.

'There are lots more things we can buy for the house as well, once we've put all the pieces together,' purred Mrs Luca.

Rose opened the last box. Inside were a cot and baby toys and even a baby with miniature clothes to dress it in.

'That's so sweet, isn't it?' said Mrs Luca. 'So sweet.'

Rose noted a catch in her voice and looked up at her. Her eyes were misty and watery. *She must be remembering the time when Victoria was born*, Rose thought. And then, without any forethought, she put her arms around Mrs Luca's waist and hugged her. She felt Mrs Luca relax and respond, and suddenly found herself holding on to her, not wanting to let go. Esme's face flashed in front of her. She could almost feel her mother's presence.

'There, there, child,' Mrs Luca murmured. 'I'm so glad you like it.'

Rose pulled away again, embarrassed and perturbed.

She didn't really know if she liked the doll's house or not. She had never seen anything like it in her life. She allowed herself to be led by Mrs Luca, who suggested that they spend the morning constructing the shell of it.

'There's no better project for a rainy day!'

Chapter 21

The doll's house stood one metre tall when they had finished constructing the outer walls. It was in the style of a mansion, like the Lucas' own house. Rose walked round it and felt quite proprietorial. She was enjoying herself and Mrs Luca seemed to be enjoying herself too, chattering away about how they could buy wallpaper and paint to decorate each of the rooms, how they could put curtains at the windows and make blankets for the beds. Mrs Luca went upstairs from time to time to check on Victoria, and came back down full of how the poor child was really not well and saying that a doctor might need to be called.

Victoria herself appeared just before lunch, complaining that she was hungry and would die of boredom if she had to stay in her room any longer. Rose was annoyed at her emergence, especially when she kept stealing Mrs Luca's attention by moaning and groaning about pains in her stomach – though they didn't stop her from demolishing a sandwich and a chocolate bar. Rose was pleasantly surprised then when Victoria gave her a neatly wrapped parcel, only to find that it was a book about England, written in English.

'I bought it with my allowance. I know it'll be a while before you can read it,' she said pointedly, 'but the pictures are nice.'

'It's such a thoughtful present, isn't it?' Mrs Luca said, beaming. 'And haven't we done well with Anna's doll's house?'

'Lovely,' smirked Victoria. 'As long as you don't expect me to play happy families with it too.'

'Talking of happy families, we must take some photos to remind Anna of her birthday. I'll fetch the camera.'

Mrs Luca swept out of the room. Victoria waited for a moment, before announcing to Rose that she had no intention of staying to have her photograph taken. Rose watched her go, wishing she could follow. Mrs Luca returned a few seconds later with Marina, and quickly masked her disappointment over her daughter's disappearance.

'We have all the time in the world to organise some

family portraits,' she said, 'but we mustn't miss this special day.'

She passed the camera to Marina and went to stand with Rose.

'Smile, miss,' Marina encouraged Rose, adopting a big smile herself and winking at her.

'Take several shots,' said Mrs Luca, 'then we can choose the best.' She stood Rose in front of her and placed her hands on her shoulders. 'Big cheese,' she said brightly.

Rose smiled, but she couldn't have felt more uncomfortable. She sighed inwardly when at last Mrs Luca declared herself satisfied and dismissed Marina. *Thank goodness that's over!*

After lunch, Victoria announced that she was well enough to join them in taking the horses out. She galloped ahead on Griffin, while Mrs Luca still insisted that Rose should attempt nothing more than a slow canter. Rose tried to show she was capable of greater things by speeding up every so often, but Mrs Luca always called her back. She took some comfort from being outside and away from the playroom where they had set up her doll's house, which had lost its charm once Victoria had joined them. Now that the rain had stopped, it was a beautiful, crisp afternoon, the sky a crystal blue broken only by a few languid white clouds. Rose breathed in the fresh air and took pleasure in the parade of autumn colours that passed by. She smiled at Mrs Luca, who showed her delight by throwing her head back and laughing out loud.

'We're having such a good day, aren't we, Anna?'

Rose nodded, and she meant it.

'There's another surprise to come when we get home,' Mrs Luca added.

The surprise was a chocolate birthday cake in the shape of a castle, complete with a princess on top.

'We had this made specially by the best baker in town,' Mrs Luca purred.

'And it was my idea,' Victoria crowed, taking a large spoonful from her plate.

Mr Luca came to join them.

'Daddy's a chocoholic, aren't you, Daddy?' Victoria said, putting her arms around him.

He nodded gruffly. 'Has it been a good day?' he asked, not addressing the question to anyone in particular.

'Perfect,' said Mrs Luca. 'Hasn't it, Anna?'

Rose nodded again, licking her lips clean. The cake was the best she had ever tasted.

'I'm glad to hear it. It cost me enough,' Mr Luca stated, as he cut himself a large piece of cake.

'And it was worth every penny to see Anna looking so happy,' Mrs Luca said sharply. 'It won't be long before she rediscovers her voice, and then she'll be able to express her gratitude to you fully.'

'Hmmph. Much good that will do me,' Mr Luca muttered.

Rose was gratified to see that he had a dollop of chocolate clinging to his moustache, which made him look slightly ridiculous. She treasured the image a little while later, when she had gone to bed and was reflecting on the day. It didn't matter how obnoxious Mr Luca might be to her now, because whenever he was, she would switch on that image to cut him down to size. *Why is he so horrid?* she wondered. *And what was he like before I arrived?* She couldn't have failed to notice that he was worried about money, and that Mrs Luca and Victoria carried on spending regardless. Was that the reason? And did he dislike her simply because she was costing him more money? Or was there a deeper reason?

Rose thought again how lucky she was to have had a father like Nicu, and pictured him sitting at the front of their wagon, alternately smoking his pipe and whistling gently. He was a giant of a man, her father, compared to Mr Luca, yet it was Mr Luca who was the real ogre – a chocolate-moustached ogre.

Rose was giggling to herself when there was a loud knock on her door. She began to get out of bed to answer it, but before she had the chance, the door flew open and Victoria barged in.

'Have you got my bracelet?' the girl demanded.

Rose didn't have a clue what Victoria was talking about. She shook her head.

'I left it on the hall table when we took the horses out, but it's not there now.' Victoria glared at Rose. 'Don't tell me you didn't see it?'

Rose adamantly shook her head again. She could hear Mrs Luca calling from downstairs, telling Victoria not to go accusing her sister.

'She's not my sister!' Victoria shouted. 'She'll never be my sister.'

Mrs Luca began to climb the stairs. 'It's probably fallen down somewhere, or you put it somewhere else and forgot.'

'I'm not stupid!' Victoria hurled at her. 'I know where I put it and it's not there now.'

'That doesn't mean it had anything to do with Anna. Leave her alone, please, and let's have a proper look for it.'

Victoria slammed the bedroom door.

'Why are you always protecting her?' Rose heard her say. 'You don't know anything about her.'

'If I don't protect her, who else will?' Mrs Luca countered.

Chapter 22

The bracelet didn't turn up. A few weeks later, another fish died. Rose was in the middle of a lesson with Mrs Conta, when they became aware of a furore outside. They went to the window, which overlooked the gardens. Mr Luca was standing with his hands behind his head as if in despair, but he was shouting. Goran was by the pond, holding a net and attempting to retrieve the dead fish from the water. Summoned by the disturbance, Mrs Luca left the house and made her way towards them. Mr Luca turned on her and blasted her with a venomous barrage of words, which were indecipherable through the closed window, but whose meaning was certainly not lost.

In that moment, Mr Luca caught sight of Rose in the window. He stared long and hard at her. Rose withered under the look of sheer animosity his pose suggested.

'Come, Anna,' said Mrs Conta. 'Back to work. There's nothing we can do to help.'

Rose found herself shaking. The teacher did her best to distract her with a comic picture book about a dog with an extreme sense of smell, but Rose couldn't concentrate. Mr Luca was blaming her for the death of his fish, she was sure of it. *Does he think I poisoned it? That I put a curse on it? Does he really believe I could do such a thing?* She wondered what else he might think to accuse her of.

'Are you paying attention, Anna?' Mrs Conta asked.

Rose shook her head. She took a piece of paper and wrote painstakingly, *fish dead not me.*

'Of course not!' exclaimed Mrs Conta as soon as she understood what Rose meant. 'What on earth makes you think anyone is blaming you?'

Mr Luca not like me, Rose wrote.

'Mr Luca is a very difficult man,' Mrs Conta said quietly. 'Very difficult. But I'm sure it's not you he's angry with. When you're a child, it's easy to think grown-ups are angry with you when in fact they're angry with everything but you.'

Rose wasn't convinced. She tried to concentrate on her lessons, but Mr and Mrs Luca's row moved indoors and she couldn't blot out the raised voices, which carried on for what seemed like hours. She was glad to be with Mrs Conta. She wasn't ready to be left on her own to cope with the fallout from the argument, and was sure the teacher would stick up for her should Mr Luca accuse her of any wrongdoing.

As soon as the last lesson was over and Mrs Conta had dismissed her with a friendly pat on the back, Rose went to her room. There were no further sounds from below, but once again she dared not go downstairs straight away. After a while, she tentatively opened her bedroom door, checked that the coast was clear and made her way to the playroom.

Her doll's house had been left untouched since her birthday. Mrs Luca hadn't at any time suggested that they might continue building it together. Rose saw no reason not to play with it. *It's my present after all, so why shouldn't I carry on with it on my own?* She couldn't help being astonished and excited all over again when she saw the sheer scale and exquisite details of the model. She resolved to make this her very own venture. It would be her first ever house!

The roof was the next thing that needed to be constructed. Rose dug out all the pieces from one of the boxes and began fitting them together. There was a plan showing the different stages, but Rose found it difficult to follow with her scant knowledge of English. She laid the pieces out on the floor and tried to marry them up with the pictures on the plan. Slowly but surely, she sorted out what went where and the roof began to take shape. Rose picked up one large section and held it above the house to check that it was correct before fixing it to the top of the wall. Just as she did so, Mrs Luca came in.

'Ah, there you are, Anna,' Mrs Luca said. Her face was unsmiling.

Rose sprang to her feet.

'I'm afraid that Mr Luca and I have decided to dispense with Mrs Conta's services. She will no longer be taking you for lessons. I shall teach you myself, when I have the time.'

Rose couldn't help but show her alarm and disappointment.

'You must realise that your lessons have been very costly for us. Mr Luca's business has run into a few problems – nothing to worry about – and we may be able to bring in a new teacher in the future. For the moment, though, it's necessary for us to reduce our expenditure. Do you understand me, Anna?'

Rose nodded her head sadly.

'I'm glad to see you're getting on with your house.

We can't have it just sitting there, can we?' Mrs Luca smiled briefly.

Rose shook her head. She was only too pleased to have Mrs Luca's approval to complete the house, especially now that it seemed as if she was going to have little else to do.

'There's one more thing, Anna.'

Rose waited, anxious once more that Mrs Luca was going to mention the dead fish and the missing bracelet.

'The stable boy is no longer in our employ, either. We've agreed that you should earn your keep by taking over from him.'

Rose gasped. She hadn't expected that. *Does it mean that the stable boy had something to do with the bracelet and the fish?* she wondered. Secretly, she couldn't help feeling cheered, because she didn't think she'd mind mucking out the horses.

Mrs Luca misinterpreted her gasp as being one of dismay. 'You should think yourself lucky,' she said shortly. 'Many young girls would do anything to be allowed to look after horses. You'll start tomorrow, after you've walked the dog, and I shall expect you to do a good job.'

She didn't wait for Rose to respond, but parted briskly.

Rose was left to struggle with her emotions. She was devastated at the news of Mrs Conta's departure. Mrs Conta had been her friend as well as her teacher, yet Rose hadn't even been allowed to say goodbye to her.

She was worried about having lessons with Mrs Luca. Theirs was a different relationship. She would never have counted Mrs Luca as a friend however much she had been showered with presents and finery by her. She was terrified too about how Mrs Luca would react when she found out about her lack of reading and writing skills, even though she had now mastered some of the basics. Mrs Conta had been pleased with her and said she was a very quick learner, but Rose doubted she had been quick enough to impress Mrs Luca. Rarely had Rose felt close to this woman who liked to speak of her as her daughter. Rose certainly didn't think of Mrs Luca as her mother, but now their relationship seemed to have undergone an inexplicable change. Mrs Luca had been abrupt with her and had treated her more like a servant than a daughter. *Was this what I was warned about*, Rose wondered, *when Marina and Goran told me to beware of upsetting my guardian? Have I upset her somehow?*

Rose was plagued again by fears that she was being held accountable for the mysterious dead fish and the missing bracelet. She wanted to find some way to plead her innocence, but how could she? In any case, she was certain that even if she were able to raise the issue she would just draw more suspicion to herself. She would have to keep her head held high, do as she was told and hope that nothing else would happen to cause more trouble.

Chapter 23

Mornings in the stables became the best part of the day for Rose, even when the weather grew colder and it rained frequently. Goran couldn't spoil them for her, either, though he tried. She did her utmost not to allow herself to be brought down by his snide comments and accusations, nor by his muttered warnings.

'You won't last here,' he said more than once. 'You don't have a cat in hell's chance. Not when her ladyship puts two and two together and comes up with the right answer. You'll be out of the door faster than I can say "good riddance".'

For a while, Rose wondered about Goran's hostility towards her, which was less understandable than Mr Luca's. In the end, all she could think of was that he didn't like her because she was a Roma, or he didn't want to share Mrs Luca's attentions.

Luckily, there was plenty to keep him occupied. It was a busy time of year in the garden, with leaves to be cleared, some vegetables to be cropped and others sown, flowers to be deadheaded and shrubs to be pruned. Mrs Luca regularly visited him to issue instructions, though it was clear Goran knew what he was doing. Rose guessed that he wouldn't want to ruin his employer's high regard for him by being seen hanging around the stables too often when he was supposed to be working. She overheard them discussing things sometimes – Goran smooth-talking and charming, Mrs Luca full of compliments and flattered by his attentions. Knowing how nasty he could be, it filled Rose with disgust to see how gullible Mrs Luca was in his company.

Rose threw herself into the tasks she had been set in the stables. She loved and understood horses, and they whinnied happily as she worked around them. It gave her a sense of triumph to be able to form a bond with Griffin and Victoria's other horse, Snooty, and she made doubly sure there was never any reason for the girl to complain about her work. Rose was grateful that Victoria was normally still in bed while she raked out the soiled bedding, washed down the concrete underneath, then piled in fresh straw.

Mrs Luca seemed in no rush to begin lessons with

her. 'I'll see if I can find time tomorrow,' she said. Or, 'There's just so much to do at the moment, but I'm sure next week will be clearer.'

Rose didn't mind. Nor did she mind the fact that she was left to her own devices so often. Mrs Luca no longer expected her company on shopping trips, and seemed more intent on buying Victoria's affections. Rose regularly overheard Mrs Luca offering her inducements like new items of clothing, the latest gadgets, facials and expensive lunches. Mother and daughter increasingly disappeared out of the house, arm in arm, laughing loudly, and stayed away for several hours.

During their absence, and with Marina's acquiescence, Rose slipped into the piano room to play the violin. Rose liked Marina. The housekeeper had told her that she had come to work for the Luca family when her husband became unreasonable and kicked her out. 'My husband was English and I moved over here to be with him, but he didn't treat me well. Mrs Luca heard about it at the church and took me in. At first, I lived as part of the family and ate meals with them. Then their housekeeper left and they said I should work for them to pay them back for their kindness. It was fair, but Mr Luca isn't very nice to me, and I was never a servant back in Romania.'

'Be very careful,' Marina warned Rose regularly about using the piano room. 'There'll be an almighty row if anyone finds you in there, and I wouldn't want to see you get into trouble.'

But as time went by, Rose became bolder, stealing moments even when she knew there was a chance Mr Luca might come back from work early, or when it was close to the hour Mrs Luca had envisaged for their return. It was only while Rose was playing that she could rediscover the person she had once been. She was delighted to find she was improving with all the practice. The bow moved more deftly from high to low, the notes were cleaner, the transitions smoother.

Nicu would have been so proud of her! It was what he had always wanted – for her to make the most of her ability. 'You're lucky to be born with a budding talent,' he used to say, 'but talent is nothing without hard work and dedication. You must strive to help that talent blossom into a beautiful flower, whose colourful petals and delightful scent will bring joy to the world.'

'Your father is such a romantic,' Esme would laugh, 'but he's right – talent should never be wasted.'

If only I'd practised harder when Papa wanted me to, Rose lamented, *but at least I'm making up for it*. What she had been lacking before was passion. She had found passion through adversity and now could feel what her father had felt when he picked up his violin and lost himself in his music.

Occasionally, when Rose paused for a break, she would wander around the room, picking up sheets of music and wondering at the strange language of circles and lines. She knew it was the language of music, but was no more able to read it than any other language. She also glanced – with no real interest – at the pictures and photographs that covered part of a wall. Until the day when, on looking more closely, she thought she recognised Mrs Luca in one of the photographs.

Rose lifted the photograph from its hook, took it to the window and wiped away the dust with the edge of a curtain. She was sure it was Mrs Luca, much younger, dark-haired and playing the grand piano. In the background, a large audience was listening, enrapt. Rose replaced the photograph and began to study the others. One appeared to be Mrs Luca as a child, with a violin in her hands. Another showed her standing in front of a piano receiving a huge bouquet of flowers.

Curiosity got the better of Rose now. She went to the door and checked that Marina was downstairs, then crept over to the chest of drawers and tentatively opened the top drawer. It was full of baby clothes, all neatly folded, many of them scarcely worn, others still with labels on. Rose opened another drawer. This one contained photograph albums. She leafed through the first album to find more images of Mrs Luca at various stages of her musical career. A second held numerous photographs of a baby girl.

To begin with, Rose thought the baby must be Victoria, though she didn't bear much resemblance. This child was dark, while Victoria was fair. Most of the photographs were portraits of the child on her own – in her cot, in her high chair, in her playpen, toddling on the lawn, playing in a nursery. Then Rose discovered a batch where the child was in Mrs Luca's arms, or holding her hand, or playing with a balloon, some with Mr Luca beside them, looking happy. Others portrayed the child with Victoria, and there were what appeared to be family shots, with Mr and Mrs Luca, Victoria and the little girl all together.

Who is this child? Rose wondered. She searched further, but although there were dozens of photographs of the girl up to the age of about two, there were none of her any older than that. Rose guessed that she must have been about three or four years younger than Victoria, the same age difference as she herself shared with Victoria.

Virtually hidden at the bottom of the drawer, Rose found several photographs of a much younger Mr Luca, a rather pretty, fair-haired woman she had never seen before, and a very young toddler who could have been Victoria.

She put the albums carefully back in the drawer, propped the violin under her chin and resumed her practice. However, she couldn't concentrate. Her mind was full of questions about the Luca family and her own place within it. Mrs Luca had clearly been a pianist of some standing, so why did the piano now sit in this room unused and covered with dust? Why was there never any music in the house? Who was the woman standing alongside Mr Luca and gazing so dotingly at baby Victoria? Most of all, who was the other girl, who, in the photographs, seemed so cherished?

Where is she now? Rose wondered.

She quietly left the room and closed the door on its secrets. She took herself off to the playroom, where the doll's house stood with its roof, floors and windows all in place, its carpets and rugs laid and some of the furniture arranged. She rummaged through the boxes until she came to the one that contained a collection of men, women, children and babies. She selected those that most resembled the Luca family, then picked out a baby and another woman. Rose found a cot, put the baby in it and placed them in the nursery. She took the man and the two women and set them in front of the house, and stood Victoria to one side.

Which one is your mother, Victoria? I don't think it's Mrs Luca.

Chapter 24

A silver jug went missing. This time, Mrs Luca questioned Rose directly.

'Anna,' she said, calling her into the dining room, 'there was a small silver jug on the shelf here, but it's not there now. Have you seen it?' She stared piercingly at Rose.

Rose shook her head vehemently.

'I won't be cross if you give it back,' Mrs Luca persisted.

Rose spread her hands open to indicate that she knew nothing about the missing jug.

'It's very strange that items have gone missing since you've been here. And that those fish have died.'

Rose shook her head, then kept shaking it.

'I believe you, Anna. This time,' Mrs Luca said, without any real conviction. 'Next time I might not.

I hope there won't *be* a next time. Go to your room now. I'm tired of dealing with a child who cannot – will not – speak. I think perhaps it's convenient for you not to speak. I don't want to see you for the rest of today.'

And then the inevitable happened. Rose was in the piano room, practising. Marina had joined her and was sitting on the piano stool, listening in awe. She was the first to see Mr Luca as his shadow fell across the floor. She leapt to her feet and turned to find her employer standing in the doorway. She tried to attract Rose's attention, but Rose was too absorbed.

'Get out,' he fired at her. 'Get out of my house!'

Marina fled.

Rose played on, eyes closed, lost in the music of her people, unaware of Mr Luca's presence. He leant against the door frame, arms folded, and waited. When, at last, Rose released herself from the web she had spun, she opened her eyes and lowered the violin. Three loud claps made her spin round.

'So you do have a talent,' said Mr Luca. 'I was beginning to wonder what I was paying for. It's a shame you use your talent to play such trashy music, though.'

Rose backed away from him, her legs trembling so hard she could barely keep upright.

'What are you doing in here?' Mr Luca asked. 'Wait, that's a stupid question, isn't it, since I'm not going to get an answer from you.'

Rose tried to steady herself by clutching the edge of the piano.

'Take your hands off that,' shouted Mr Luca.

Rose yelped and dropped her hand by her side, which brought a sinister smirk to her guardian's face.

'Did you hear that?' he said. 'A sound escaped your lips. There must be more where that came from. Tell me, what are you doing in here?'

Rose opened her mouth. She wanted to plead with him to let her go. She wanted to tell him that she meant no harm, but no words came.

'What will my wife say when I tell her you've broken into her shrine and soiled one of her sacred instruments with such trashy music – if it's even worthy of the name "music"? I don't think she'll be very happy. I don't think she'll be very happy at all. She's not someone to upset, my wife. She's already begun to question your place here. That's what she does. She has projects. They make her feel good for a while, and then she tires of them when they don't meet her high expectations.

You're one of her projects, but not one she would have chosen if it hadn't been for the accident. Even my wife wouldn't be desperate enough to choose a Gypsy. She was driven by guilt, you see. I don't share that guilt, but I want to keep my wife happy. And now look what you've done.' Mr Luca was speaking quietly, but his tone was ominous.

Rose didn't know what he was talking about any more. She was desperate to escape.

'What should I do with you, eh?' Mr Luca asked.

He stared straight into her eyes and she felt her heart freeze. He drummed his fingers on the door frame for what seemed like minutes on end. Then he laughed.

'Get down to the kitchen and make me a cup of tea,' he ordered. 'Later, you will play for my wife.'

He stood aside to let her go. Rose tore out of the room and down the stairs, slipping on the marble hall floor and twisting her ankle. Pain shot up her leg, but it was nothing compared to the terrible thumping of her heart. She was petrified that Mr Luca would follow her. As soon as she reached the kitchen, she ran inside and pushed the door to behind her.

She didn't know where anything was. She found what she thought must be a kettle, though it was nothing like Esme's kettle. She filled it with water and opened one cupboard after another in search of tea. She began to panic when she couldn't find it, and the kettle didn't seem to be working. She flicked a switch and, to her relief, it sprang into action. She searched the cupboards again, then looked into a row of jars that lined the back of one of the worktops. At last, she found one that contained tea leaves.

As she began a new search, this time for a teapot, she heard voices. Mrs Luca and Victoria had returned. Within seconds, they had entered the kitchen.

'What are you doing in here?' Mrs Luca asked sharply. 'Where's Marina?'

'Now we know what Anna gets up to while we're away,' smirked Victoria. 'She helps herself to tea – and whatever else she can find, probably.'

The kettle behind Rose issued a tiny whistling noise that grew louder and louder.

'You really are the most frustrating child,' Mrs Luca fumed. 'I know you can speak. They told me at the hospital that you're perfectly able, and yet you stand there like some dumb animal.'

Rose was worried the kettle was going to explode.

'Is your pet not coming up to scratch?' Mr Luca appeared behind them.

'Ha, ha, good joke, Daddy,' laughed Victoria.

A sudden snap and the kettle went quiet.

'She's making me a cup of tea. Would you like one?' Mr Luca offered.

'Will you please explain what's going on?' demanded Mrs Luca.

'It seems we have a musical genius in our midst,' he replied.

'Don't!' Mrs Luca warned him sharply.

'But I didn't mean you, darling. I meant our Gypsy friend here. It seems she's a bit of a whizz on the fiddle.'

'Ha, ha, another good joke, Daddy. Do you get it, Mummy?'

'No, I don't,' Mrs Luca replied angrily.

'I'll reveal all over a nice cup of tea, provided our new housekeeper can produce it sometime this week. Later on, I shall ask her to entertain us.'

He guided his wife and daughter out of the kitchen, leaving Rose aghast as she took in the meaning of his words. *Does he really intend that I should play for Mrs Luca? For all of them?* She was in such dread at the thought that she dropped a cup on the floor as she assembled the tea service. She picked up the pieces, fighting back tears, and stood up to see Goran staring at her through the window.

Chapter 25

Rose was sent back to the kitchen after she had served tea and told to stay there while her future was discussed. She was to scrub clean a bowlful of newly picked potatoes that Goran had left for their dinner, and to sweep and polish the floor. Rose couldn't help overhearing raised voices through the half-open door. She wondered what fate had in store for her and considered riding off on one of the horses, but had no idea where she might go. Besides, Goran was lurking and would be sure to stop her. It occurred to her too that she might be sent away as a punishment, and then what would she do?

Victoria came in while Rose was sweeping the floor.

'Can you hear them?' she asked. 'They're at each other hammer and tongs because of you.'

She waited to see Rose's reaction before continuing.

'The thing is that Mummy – well, actually, she's not Mummy at all, though she tries so hard to be, just like she did with you, but that's only because she felt sorry for you – Mummy was a concert pianist and quite famous back home, apparently. But she stopped playing because she lost a baby and discovered she couldn't have any more, and that sort of upset her. Do you know, it was born on November the twentieth? Funny that. I'm not enough for her because I'm not her child. And now, well, now you've brought it all back to her by trespassing into her shrine.'

Rose carried on sweeping, slowly, methodically, and avoided looking up.

'You'll wear a hole in the floor if you keep brushing the same bit,' Victoria sniggered. 'Here, will this make it more worthwhile?'

She grabbed a jar and tipped it upside down. Sugar spilled in all directions.

'That'll teach you to come here and cause so much trouble. We were fine until you arrived and put a curse on everything.'

With that, Victoria flounced out of the room.

Rose had never been exposed to such hatred before – not even from those people in her homeland who complained about the presence of Roma in their towns and villages, not even from the police who sometimes moved them on. She questioned how she could possibly continue to live under the same roof as someone who despised her so much. Yet she was certain there was worse to come.

It was as she had guessed: Victoria was not Mrs Luca's child. *Who is her mother, then?* Rose supposed she must be dead. *Is that why Victoria behaves the way she does?* Victoria was spoilt, but was she really loved by either Mrs Luca or her father? As for Mrs Luca, she must have been devastated at the loss of her child, Rose thought.

She swept the sugar into a pile and searched for a dustpan and brush. She found them at the bottom of a cupboard and was about to take hold of them when something shiny caught her eye, something nestling at the bottom of a pile of dusters that she had accidentally disturbed. She was going to ignore it when a little voice in her head told her to see what it was. She lifted the corners of the dusters, and there was the missing silver jug. She let go of them as quickly as if she had been scalded, seized the dustpan and brush and slammed the cupboard door shut.

It was Marina all the time! Marina, who led me to believe that she was my friend! Marina is the thief! Rose began to brush savagely at the sugar, not caring that some of it

165

scattered. She felt more friendless than ever. She now knew who the culprit was, yet the knowledge didn't help. What could she do with it? If she revealed where she had found the jug, who was going to believe her? She would surely make things worse for herself, and Mr and Mrs Luca would simply demand that she return the bracelet as well.

Rose suddenly gasped. *Is the bracelet under the dusters as well?* She hadn't thought to check. *Should I look now?*

Dropping the dustpan and brush, she dashed to the cupboard, opened the door, paused to make sure nobody was coming and picked up the dusters. The bracelet wasn't there, just the silver jug, staring at her accusingly. She hurriedly returned the dusters to their place, covering the jug completely. *Did Marina take the bracelet with her when she left the house*, Rose wondered, *or did she hide it somewhere else?*

Rose didn't have time to dwell on it any longer, because Mrs Luca came into the kitchen.

'Stop what you're doing, Anna,' she said. 'You will play for me now.'

Mrs Luca's voice was frigid, her face haunted. She gripped the doorknob, as if using it to steady herself. Rose wanted something of her own to hang on to.

She followed Mrs Luca into the dining room. Mr Luca was sitting at the head of the table. The violin was on the table in front of him. He smiled at her and waved the bow in the air – to taunt her, Rose felt.

'I'm looking forward to this,' he said. 'Our own private performance – even if at the moment all you can play is that gutter trash.'

'Leave her,' said Mrs Luca without emotion. 'How can you expect her to perform if you abuse her?'

'I can expect it because I pay for her,' Mr Luca snapped.

Mrs Luca shot him a warning glance, then picked up the violin. She held it out to Rose.

'Here,' she said. 'Let me see what you can do.'

She took the bow from her husband and gave it to Rose.

Rose lifted the violin under her chin and placed the bow on the strings. Her mind was numb. She couldn't think of any tunes. Her hands felt as if they were wearing boxing gloves, the ones that hung from a hook in Uncle Aleksandar's wagon, a souvenir of the days when he could take on any young whippersnapper and win. She felt like a total novice, but saw the impatience in Mr Luca's face and forced herself to begin.

The bow grated as if it were covered with barbs. The

strings seemed unwilling to harmonise. Rose gritted her teeth. *I'm doing my best, and if my best isn't good enough, so what? What am I supposed to be proving? Why is Mr Luca so keen for me to impress his wife?*

She relaxed a little as soon as she had made up her mind that she didn't care. And then the music came to her – her father's favourite reel, one that she and Rani had danced to wildly when they were younger, while Esme tinkered on the accordion.

After she had played the final note, Rose dropped the violin to her side. She knew she hadn't played particularly well, and though she didn't care what they thought, she still waited anxiously for the response. Her future depended on it, she was certain.

'You can go back to your chores now,' said Mrs Luca. 'And don't you *ever* go into my room again.'

Chapter 26

Mrs Luca added to Rose's list of chores. She showed her displeasure that Rose had 'led Marina astray' by making her take over as many of Marina's duties as she deemed her able to perform.

'I'll have to do the cooking myself for the time being – which is more than a nuisance – until we can find a suitable and trustworthy replacement for Marina. You'll do the washing, cleaning and the preparation for our meals, as well as your stable duties. In return, I'll teach you how to play the violin properly. My husband has some notion that you might have considerable talent in that direction. Personally, I have my doubts, but we shall see.'

Mrs Luca drew up a timetable for Rose to follow. She would spend an hour to two hours each day teaching her classical music, and Rose was to spend a minimum of a further two hours practising on her own. There were to be no other lessons – not that Mrs Luca had ever bothered with them in the end, Rose reflected. What Rose couldn't understand was why they thought the music lessons were worthwhile. They seemed to have given up on her over everything else, and had even told her that from now on she would eat on her own in the kitchen, just as Marina used to.

'If the time comes when we feel we can trust you, then we may change our minds and treat you as one of the family again,' said Mrs Luca. 'Until then, this will be your punishment. You should count yourself lucky we're allowing you to keep your bedroom.'

Mrs Luca gave Rose permission to continue playing with her doll's house, because of the money that had already been spent on it. However, with all her new duties and music lessons, it was difficult to find time for it. Besides, she grew to despise its sterile opulence, which too closely resembled the Luca mansion. She was only happy when she was outside with Crumble or working with the horses. She was still allowed to ride the ponies, provided that Mrs Luca or Victoria went with her.

'Now that the stable boy has gone, there's no one else to exercise them,' said Mrs Luca, 'so think yourself lucky.'

Rose didn't think herself lucky at all. She had grown in the months that she had been living with the Luca family and the ponies were far too small for her now. She felt ridiculous perched on top of them.

Her music lessons with Mrs Luca were relentless in their pursuit of excellence. Mrs Luca constantly criticised; Rose's elbow was too high, her chin was at the wrong angle, she was slouching, her bowing was too laboured or too vigorous, she had no sense of rhythm, her timing was out, she may be good at Gypsy music but she would never, ever be good enough to play classical. At the end of each lesson, Rose was exhausted, yet she had numerous chores to do before going on to practise by herself. Mrs Luca kept a strict eye on her to make sure that she played for the full two hours at least, opening the door every so often to comment on what she was hearing.

What Mrs Luca didn't know was that she had lit a fire in Rose, a fire that was smouldering beneath the surface, ready to explode into red-hot flames. Every criticism Rose had to endure fanned the fire and added to her determination to prove her guardian wrong. *I'll be the best I can be in spite of Mrs Luca, not because of her,* she determined. And it was the memory of her father that kept her going when she was ready to drop.

Little by little, Rose began to appreciate the structure and discipline of the classical pieces Mrs Luca drilled her in. The melodies drifted through her and produced a welcome feeling of calm, especially when she was practising alone in her bedroom.

Some weeks after the start of her lessons, Rose came back from mucking out the stables to hear notes being played on a piano. At first, she thought it was the radio, but she quickly realised that the notes were random and out of tune. She crept upstairs to her room and was surprised to find that the sounds were coming from Mrs Luca's 'shrine'.

Later that day, a man arrived at the house. Rose answered the door to be informed that he was the piano tuner. Mrs Luca, looking uncomfortable, hurried him upstairs while shooing Rose back to the kitchen.

After that, it was no secret that Mrs Luca was playing the piano again. She disappeared into her piano room for hours on end. Through the closed door came the strains of classical pieces that Rose began to recognise because they were the same as those she was being taught to play on the violin. Rose couldn't help but admire her guardian's courage at finally coming to terms with the blows life had dealt her and moving on. Rose understood some of what she must be going through – the reconciliation of her life as it used to be with the terrible twists and turns of fate. It was something Rose would have to go through herself one day, when she was ready. She wasn't ready yet, though. Her pain was still too raw. The events that had gatecrashed her own life were still too recent. How long ago was the fateful day when she had lost everything that was dear to her? Almost a year? Over a year?

The seasons had changed around Rose. It was dark and sometimes there was a thick frost when she set off with Crumble on wintry mornings. The cold didn't bother her; she was used to that from living in their wagon, though in the depths of winter, Nicu and Esme had always found temporary accommodation in modern trailers or rented houses, where there were gas heaters to keep them warm. During her walks, she loved looking at the frost-covered cobwebs picked out by the moon and hanging like diamond-encrusted lace from gateposts and fences and trees. She loved the crunch of leaves underfoot, and watched her breath spiralling away into the air like smoke from a chimney.

Rose hoped it would snow, but the weather stayed relatively mild. She reminisced about the snowball fights with Rani and the other Roma children, and shivered at the memory of ice trickling slowly down her neck. She so missed the company of friends and cousins. Even when Mrs Luca had first brought her to the house, even when she had made an effort to be nice to her, she had never once suggested that Rose might like to meet other children. Her hope had been that Victoria would befriend her and that that would suffice, but Victoria had different ideas.

The spring brought its own delights. Rose watched snowdrops pushing up through the undergrowth and then buds blossoming on the trees. In the fields surrounding the Lucas' land, lambs were toddling on unsteady legs and demanding milk from their mothers. Birds were flighty in their search for a nesting partner and their chorus roused the dawn.

Rose often stood by the stile for moments on end, staring around her, remembering her family, and wishing she could disappear beyond the horizon to find herself back home. The relentless routine of her days inside the mansion was like a straitjacket on her life, but at the same time it was also what kept her together. She rarely had the opportunity to dwell on her circumstances and where they might be leading. She performed her duties to the best of her ability – even though that was never quite good enough for Mrs Luca – and she was able to immerse herself in her music more profoundly as the sounds she produced became acceptable to her own ears.

She was regularly left alone in the house now that Marina had gone. Mrs Luca compensated for the hours she spent teaching Rose by spoiling Victoria more than ever. While they were gone, Goran was left in charge. Rose never knew when he might put his head through a window to check on her and make a snide comment, or to demand tea and biscuits. He didn't come inside – Rose thought perhaps he wasn't allowed to – and she was glad about that, but she was always relieved when Mrs Luca returned to remove the malice that he seemed to represent.

Late one afternoon, having finished all her chores and wanting a break from her violin practice, Rose chose to do some more work on the doll's house, since there was nothing else for her to do. She would, however, stop following the instructions and design things to please herself. *I'm going to change the colour scheme from pastels to bright shades*, she thought mischievously to herself, *and I'm going to turn the servants into lords and ladies, and the other way round*. She opened the door to the playroom and froze on the threshold.

The doll's house was in ruins. The roof had been pushed in, the walls had collapsed, the garden furniture was smashed and the contents of the boxes were strewn across the playroom floor. Rose bent down to pick up one of the model people. It looked as if it had been trodden on. She lifted up a roof panel to see what the damage was like inside. What she found there filled her with yet more dismay. It was Victoria's bracelet.

Rose dropped the roof panel and ran from the room. If anyone found her there, they would believe that she had destroyed the house. The truth dawned on her, however, that regardless of where she was or what she did, the same conclusion would be reached. She would be guilty in everyone's eyes.

At least I can take away the 'proof' that I'm a thief, she suddenly thought. She stopped and retraced her steps, part of her hoping that when she opened the door this time the house would have miraculously repaired itself. It hadn't, of course, and the bracelet was still sitting under the roof, in the toy bath. Rose snatched it quickly and put it in her pocket. As she did, she noticed a dirty mark on the beige playroom carpet. It was part of a heel print – a muddy heel print.

The front door clattered open.

'Anna! Where are you, Anna? Mummy wants a cup of tea.'

Rose fled from the room again. She steadied herself as she reached the top of the stairs. It felt as if the bracelet was burning a hole in her pocket. She wondered if its shape could be spotted through her clothes, or if it could be heard clinking.

Victoria was standing at the bottom of the stairs, looking up. 'I suppose you've been getting up to mischief,' she said, as Rose made her way down.

Rose shook her head. *Please don't let her see where I've come from.*

Mrs Luca was pushing through the front door, laden with shopping.

'Help me put these things away, please, Anna,' she said, 'and put the kettle on.'

Rose hurried to help her.

'I hope you've been practising hard while we've been out,' said Mrs Luca, walking ahead of Rose into the kitchen. Then she stopped in the doorway, turned round and looked at her searchingly. 'Are you all right? You look as if you've seen a ghost.'

Chapter 27

Mr Luca came home in a foul temper that evening. From the moment he entered the house, slamming the door behind him, Rose feared something bad had happened and that it would affect her in some way. She understood very quickly that another fish had died, but there was more than that. From the snatches of loud conversation she was able to hear, it seemed Mr Luca's business ventures were collapsing around him, and that the worst of it could be traced back to the time when 'Anna' had appeared in their lives. She went about her duties in the kitchen, doing everything she was told as efficiently as she could and trying to keep as low a profile as possible.

Rose could not, however, escape the lash of Mr Luca's tongue when she served the family with dinner.

'So how's our little Gypsy girl today?' he asked. 'Still enjoying life at my expense, are we?'

Victoria sniggered.

There was no attempt by Mrs Luca to protect Rose this time.

'How have you managed it, eh? How have you managed to put a curse on this family? I never believed in that sort of rubbish until you came along, but I can't find any other explanation. The fish? That's an easy one. They innocently open their mouths and – hey presto! – you pop in something a little bit poisonous. Result? The fish go belly up. The missing bits and pieces? I'm sure we'll find your hiding places somewhere in the house if we search hard enough. My business interests? That's more difficult to put a finger on, but don't think I didn't see you staring out of the window at me no sooner than you'd arrived here.' He paused and took a large gulp of wine.

'Don't you think you've had enough, darling?' Mrs Luca said quietly.

'Yes, I have had enough!' Mr Luca slammed his fist down on the table. 'I've had enough of your projects, and I've had enough of this particular project. Just because her family saw fit to stick their wagon in front of my car and kill themselves, does it mean I have to pay with everything I've got?' Then he said, more quietly, 'Don't you think I've already suffered for it every minute of every day since?'

Victoria turned pale. Mrs Luca lowered her head. Silence followed, a silence during which Rose took in the meaning of his words – words that made no sense at first, but then made all too much sense. If ever she had wanted to howl with pain, it was now. She dropped the plate she was carrying and ran from the room, from the house.

He killed them! He killed them! A voice screamed in Rose's head, over and over. *Esme, Nicu, Rani – he killed them all. It was his fault. How could he blame them?* Without warning, she heard once more the hideous screech of metal against wood, relived the moment when the whole of her world was smashed apart.

Rose had no idea where she would go, but she had to get away. She headed for the stables. Her first thought was to take one of the ponies, but then she saw Victoria's horse, Griffin, gazing out at her over his stable door. She ran over to him, stroked him gently and opened the latch. She grabbed a crate from close by, stood on it and clambered on to his back. He whinnied loudly, excited perhaps at the possibility of a gallop after dark. All she had to do was nudge him with her knees and he responded. He trotted out of the stable. She leant over his neck to show him which direction to take, urging him to go fast, using every movement of her body to convey her intentions.

'Hey! Where d'you think you're going? Stop!'

It was Goran. Nothing on earth would make her stop for him. He had worked against her since her arrival. The heel print in the playroom was his, she was sure of it. While she had been practising the violin, he had entered the house and created mischief. It was he who had poisoned Mr Luca's precious koi carp. It all fitted into place now. He didn't like her because of who she was, not because of anything she had done. He didn't like her because she had stolen Mrs Luca's attention from him. He would do everything in his power to get rid of her.

And Goran hadn't finished with her yet. He was saddling up one of the other horses and coming after her. *Why can't he just let me go? What more does he want from me?* Rose dug her heels into Griffin's sides, willing him to gallop faster. They left the road and set off across the fields. She was exhilarated and terrified at the same time. In her heart, she was riding to freedom, while her head told her it was impossible – she knew she would be caught and taken back. But at least she could stay defiant until the end.

Moonlight caught the top of a hedge that loomed up ahead and stretched the length of the field. Rose could see no other way through. She had jumped hedges in the past, but not on a horse she didn't know, not at night. It was difficult in the darkness to tell how high the hedge was. She looked around. Goran was gaining on her, shouting at her not to be an idiot and to give herself up. Rose faced forward again. *I'm not just going to wait for him. He'll have to catch me. I'm going to attempt the hedge – after all, what's the worst that can happen?*

She wrapped her arms round Griffin's neck as tightly as she could, then willed him onward, her legs clamped to his sides. The hedge was getting closer and closer. Too late, Rose realised that it was too high. She felt Griffin's fear as his head lurched back, his legs buckled and his body lunged to the left. She tried to hold on, but she wasn't strong enough. As Griffin juddered to a halt, Rose lost her grip completely and was catapulted through the air like a rag doll.

She hit the earth and lay there, her breath punched out of her. Moments later, a grey shadow appeared and hovered above her, before it spun away into nothingness.

Chapter 28

Soft white sheets. Dim lights. Rose tried to keep her eyes open, but they seemed so determined to close. She could sense movement to her right, but couldn't turn her head. It felt as if someone had attached a heavy weight to it. Something stirred in her memory, something to do with waking up in a strange place and finding blood on the sheets. Something to do with an accident. She struggled to sit up. Someone restrained her. She tried to say something. No sound came.

'You need to rest, Anna.'

The voice was familiar. The name wasn't.

'You took a nasty bang on the head. Nothing serious that a few days in bed won't cure, the doctor says. I don't know what you were thinking of, taking a horse out without a saddle.'

Rose started to recall what had happened.

'You could have killed yourself, and the horse.'

Killed yourself and the horse. Killed Nicu and Esme and Rani and the horse. Poor Philippos . . .

Rose just managed to turn her head. Mrs Luca was sitting next to her. When she realised that this woman who had destroyed her family was holding her hand, Rose yanked it away and pulled the bedclothes around herself.

'About what my husband said,' Mrs Luca said quietly. 'He had had some very bad news, and rather a lot to drink. We wouldn't want you to get the wrong impression. The accident wasn't our fault, do you understand? It was just that – an accident – but ever since both of us have struggled to come to terms with it, believe me. And because such a terrible thing had happened to you, we wanted to make sure you had all the very best in life from that point onward. We didn't want you to suffer.'

She paused to let Rose take in the import of her words.

'You've made it very difficult for us to make amends. Your behaviour has led us to deal with you harshly, yet we began with such good intentions. So many things have gone wrong since you arrived, and what you did to the doll's house was unforgivable. I spent so much effort and money on it, only for you to repay me by wrecking it.'

She paused again, watching for Rose's reaction. Rose closed her eyes. There was no reaction she could give that would change anything. She heard Mrs Luca stand up and sigh.

'I'll leave you to rest now. I'll leave you to think about how you can help us all move on.' Mrs Luca walked to the door and said stiffly, 'You know, you're a very lucky girl, Anna. If it hadn't been for Goran, you might still be lying outside in the cold and wet. He may have saved your life. You should be eternally grateful to him.'

She closed the door behind her, leaving Rose to continue recalling the events that had led up to her taking the horse and what had occurred afterwards. Her mind flashed back to the shadowy figure hovering over her in the darkness like an angel of death. Goran was triumphant, untouchable. He could make her life hell and nobody would notice, just as they wouldn't notice the muddy heel print on the playroom floor.

A shockwave went through her when she suddenly remembered the bracelet hidden in the pocket of her trousers. *Has it been discovered? Mrs Luca didn't mention it*. Rose struggled to get out of bed to check, but her head was thumping too hard, and she was fearful someone might catch her. She closed her eyes again.

Sometime later, Mrs Luca came back into the bedroom, accompanied by the doctor. He examined Rose and pronounced that she was doing well and would be as right as rain in a couple of days. She had sustained a mild concussion, but there was nothing to be concerned about.

'Better stay away from horses until you're a bit bigger,' he said. 'They can be dangerous animals.'

Rose didn't understand all the words, but enough to know what he meant, especially when Mrs Luca said, 'Don't worry, doctor. We shan't be letting Anna near a horse again. She's far too precious to us.'

A visit from Victoria followed. She slipped through the door and closed it silently behind her.

'What the hell do you think you were doing taking Griffin?' she hissed. 'Don't you think you've done enough damage without stealing my horse as well? You could have broken his legs trying to go over that hedge, and then we'd have had to have him put down. Do you think that's all right? Do you?'

186

Victoria tore the bedcovers out of Rose's hands.

'Don't just lie there like some poor injured animal,' she fumed. 'What's Daphne said about it? I suppose she's told you that you're a naughty little girl and not to do it again. Well, I think you're an evil little girl and I wish you'd go away and stay away. I wish you'd just leave our house and never come back. But no. Daddy seems to think he can make some money out of you, so instead we've all got to tread softly, softly with you and not upset you too much. Ha! Nobody cares if *I'm* upset. Nobody cares that it was my horse you stole and my bracelet. And I don't believe it was Daddy's fault about your family's accident. I bet it was all their fault.'

Rose couldn't take any more. She bolted out of bed and threw herself at Victoria, pushing her and pummelling her with her fists. Victoria was too strong. She caught hold of Rose's arms and shoved her backwards.

'Don't you dare touch me,' she hissed. 'Don't you ever touch me again. You're not my sister and I hate you more than anything I've ever hated in my life!'

Chapter 29

As soon as Rose was well enough, she resumed her duties in the kitchen. She wasn't allowed to go near the horses. That was considered too much of a risk, and she wasn't trusted not to 'do something silly' again. She was made to practise the violin ever more frequently, sometimes up to six hours a day, until she began to loathe it.

Rose gradually understood what Victoria had meant when she said that her father thought he could make money out of her. It seemed he was planning some sort of comeback tour for his wife, and that Rose was to be part of the tour.

'Why anyone would pay good money to come and hear you, I don't know,' Victoria said more than once. 'I wouldn't go and watch some kid scratching away on a violin.'

If Mrs Luca overheard, she scolded her. 'The one thing we can say about Anna is that she has a very great talent.'

'Which you're going to exploit,' Victoria retorted, changing her tune.

'Which we're going to show to the world,' replied Mrs Luca. 'And people will be paying their money to listen to me, not Anna.'

'It's good for Daddy, anyhow, that he's found a way to get his money back.'

'I'm sure you'll enjoy helping to spend it again,' Mrs Luca said.

'You're the one who's always taking me out shopping because it makes you feel better.'

'Don't be so unkind, darling. You know I just want you to be happy.'

Rose couldn't bear to listen to them. This wasn't what families were supposed to be like. Families were supposed to love and support each other. They were supposed to stick together, not backbite and fight. Nicu wasn't a confrontational man, but he wouldn't have tolerated Victoria's behaviour towards her parents. Equally, he and Esme always ensured that life for Rose and Rani was filled with laughter, even when they were cold, or short of money, or being asked to move on by the police. There was no such thing as fun in the Luca household. Rose doubted there was any such thing as love, either.

It was only when Mrs Luca told her the tour they were planning was to take place in their home country that Rose began to feel excited at the prospect. Up until then, she had cringed at the very thought of it. She had never in her wildest dreams imagined she would see her home country again. Now, she convinced herself that somehow her family would discover her whereabouts once she was there. Uncle Aleksandar and Aunt Mirela or their Roma friends would find her, she was sure of it. In darker moments, though, she told herself there wasn't even the slightest possibility of being reunited with them. *Why would they come anywhere near a classical music concert given by a middle-aged gadje woman?* Nevertheless, it cheered her to know that at some point in the near future she would be treading on home soil for the first time in many months. Every day Rose waited to be told that all the arrangements had been made for the trip and that they would be departing shortly.

Mrs Luca had started allowing her into the piano room so that they could practise together. She had changed the room around. The walls were now covered

190

with more certificates of achievement and newspaper articles about concerts she had given – perhaps to provide inspiration, Rose thought. The curtains were now kept open, but the room was still a dreary, soulless place.

Mrs Luca would sit herself down at the piano and instruct Rose to stand to one side, facing her. She was fastidious about Rose's posture, picking up on every slouch of the shoulders or drop of the head, even after the lengthiest practice session. The focus was entirely on two pieces of music, which Rose was to learn to play faultlessly, accompanied by Mrs Luca. One would be slotted in towards the end of Mrs Luca's recital, the second would serve as an encore.

'Two pieces will be enough for people to be impressed by what you're capable of. That's plenty for you to work on, and we wouldn't want anyone to think we're exploiting you,' Mrs Luca asserted. 'Besides, they'll be there to see me.'

Rose wondered what they planned to say about her. She was dismayed at the thought of an audience of people gawping at her just because she was a Gypsy girl playing classical music. The jumble of emotions she had to deal with kept her awake at night, leaving her exhausted during the day. She was permanently on edge over her household duties, which she never seemed to be able to complete to the family's satisfaction.

Victoria delighted in inventing tasks for her to do and making her wait on her hand and foot. Mr Luca was absent from the house more frequently, and when he returned he was invariably in a bad mood. Mrs Luca was stern and unsmiling, locked in her own thoughts.

Just when Rose began to suspect that the talk about a tour had been nothing more than talk, Mr Luca called her into his study and announced that they would be leaving for Romania in four weeks' time.

'You'd better shape up,' he told her. 'My wife has a significant reputation to maintain. I would have liked to say that you'll be the icing on the cake, the jewel in the crown, but I'll never be able to think of you as anything other than the dirt beneath my shoe – which is where you'll go back to once the tour is over. There'll be no trying to outshine my wife, do you understand? You'll deliver your piece, take your applause, then slip back into oblivion. This is all about the revival of my wife's career as a concert pianist.'

Rose nodded meekly. Inside, she was raging. It wasn't about the revival of his wife's career, but about saving this man from his financial ruin. *This man who killed my family. This man who insults me time and time again, however much he claims to have suffered himself.* This man who, with all his wealth and arrogance, was unworthy of sharing the same air as her family. She wished all his beloved fish would die. She wished he would lose his fortune and wind up having to sleep on the streets, wrapped up in cardboard against the freezing cold. Then she could enjoy passing him by in her own warm, toasty wagon and calling out, 'I'll never be able to think of you as anything other than the dirt beneath my shoe.'

Rose was ashamed of herself for thinking such things. Were these the kinds of terrible thoughts that living with Mr Luca and his family had driven her to?

Chapter 30

The days began to fly past now that a departure date had been set. There seemed to be so much to do. They were going to be away for a month, and Mrs Luca insisted that everything should be scrubbed, polished, washed, ironed and aired before they left.

'We don't want to come back and have all the house-work to do then,' she said. 'I only wish we had some proper help.'

'If the tour is successful and my business meetings go well, then you shall,' said Mr Luca.

Victoria made herself scarce while there were chores to be done – not that she helped much anyway. 'I have to catch up with my friends before we leave,' she said. 'I won't be seeing them for ages.'

Rose had hoped Victoria would be staying at home rather than accompanying them to Romania. She dreaded being closeted with her in hotels for a whole month.

When the day finally came for them to leave, Rose could hardly contain her excitement and anxiety. *I'm going home!* She took Crumble for his walk as usual, but made a huge fuss of him, telling him with her hugs that she was sorry she would never see him again. She sneaked back via the stables and stroked the horses goodbye. In her head, she said farewell to her bedroom and to every other part of the house in turn, in order to convince herself that she was leaving them for ever.

Mrs Luca hurried around, issuing instructions and making last-minute arrangements with Goran for the upkeep of the house and gardens. She invited him inside to take receipt of keys and go through a list of jobs that would need to be done in their absence. She left him in the kitchen while she rushed about, until a shout of dismay brought everyone running into the hall.

'It's my gold brooch, the one my mother gave me,' Mrs Luca cried. 'It's gone!'

Rose began to shake. *Surely not today? Surely he can't sabotage things just when I'm about to go home?*

'I never travel without it, and I never put it anywhere except in my jewellery box,' Mrs Luca said, completely distraught.

Goran's eyes rested on Rose and a faint smirk licked at the corners of his lips.

'Where is it, Anna?' Victoria came straight to the point.

'I must have it. It brings me good luck,' Mrs Luca whimpered.

'Good luck?' Mr Luca scoffed. 'Since when has it brought you or any of us good luck? It certainly didn't bring us good luck last time we travelled.'

All eyes were now on Rose. She shook her head over and over again. Tears began to spill down her cheeks. *Why can't they see that it's not me?* She turned to Goran and pointed at him accusingly, but knew immediately it was a mistake. Goran let out a howl of laughter.

'Me?' he said. 'You think I had something to do with it? Now listen, miss, you can't come here and start accusing people who've worked their butts off for this family for years and never caused a moment's trouble. You'll be accusing me of killing the koi carp next!'

There was an awkward silence.

Mr Luca stared hard at the gardener, his lips tightening. 'We haven't got time for this,' he said firmly. 'You'll have to go without it, darling. We'll deal with this when we return.'

'Please, Anna,' begged Mrs Luca, 'if you've taken it, please let me have it.'

'Shall I go and check her room?' asked Victoria.

'Haven't I just said that we haven't got time?' Mr Luca flared. 'If it's in her room, it'll still be there when we get back. At this rate, we'll miss our flight, and then the whole tour will go pear-shaped.'

He hurried them out of the house, Mrs Luca still arguing that she didn't want to go without her brooch, and Victoria muttering to Rose about her thieving little fingers and the new upset she'd caused. Rose kept her head down and focused on thoughts of her home. She cast a glance at the Luca mansion with its daunting frontage as the car began to pull away.

Goran was standing on the steps, looking for all the world as if he owned the place. When he saw her looking, he delved into his pocket, pulled out something shiny, dangled it briefly, then put it away again. It was the bracelet, Rose was sure of it. Goran must have found it after she'd fallen from the horse. Now he had all the 'proof' he needed that she was the thief.

The journey to the airport was full of silences. Rose stared out of the window at people going about their day-to-day lives. She had met so few of them in this country that wasn't her own. She had seen so little of the countryside and the towns they were passing through now. She had lived as a virtual prisoner once Mrs Luca had tired of taking her out. Their home had been her home, yet she had lived there as an unwelcome stranger. Rose felt better just being away from it, and opened herself up to the call of freedom. She wouldn't allow any doubts to settle in her mind. *As long as I stay strong, something good will happen.* She thought about Aunt Mirela and the way people queued to have their fortunes told. She remembered the crystal ball and wondered what she would see if she stared into its depths. *As long as I stay strong, something good will happen*, she repeated to herself.

Her journey was going in reverse. Just as she had flown out of Romania, landed in England and been driven to Mr and Mrs Luca's house, now she was being driven away from there to fly out of England and into Romania. *If only I could reverse everything else*, she thought wistfully, but she refused to dwell on it.

At last, Rose saw signs for the airport and breathed a sigh of relief that soon she would be able to escape the oppressive atmosphere of the car. Mrs Luca had scarcely said a word apart from expressing her apprehension at flying without her brooch. Victoria had her eyes closed, though Rose doubted she was asleep. Mr Luca grunted occasionally and cursed at the amount of traffic, but otherwise said nothing.

Arriving at the airport, the driver dropped them off

outside the departure area and helped them unload their baggage. There were crowds of people everywhere. Rose was worried about getting lost and kept close to Mrs Luca, until they passed through into a special lounge for frequent flyers, where it was quieter and there was space to sit comfortably. Victoria clung on to her father, quickly persuading him to explore the shops. For once, she didn't come back with anything, and while they waited Mr Luca grumbled about the state of his finances and the fact that they were being forced to travel economy class with the 'great unwashed'.

When their flight was eventually called, Rose could hardly stand up she was so tense. She was glad Mrs Luca had long since ceased to cluck over her and allowed her to make her own way on to the plane. The seats were in blocks of three this time. The Luca family sat together and Rose was across the aisle. She fastened her seat belt, rested her head back and watched the other passengers jostling and chattering as they found their places and loaded their luggage overhead. Many were Romanians, excited about going back home. A few were English, setting off on their holidays. Rose tuned in as much as possible to what they were saying in order to block out the complaints from Mr Luca, who was moaning bitterly about the crowding, the lack of legroom and the noisy children.

As soon as the plane took off, Rose closed her eyes so that the woman beside her wouldn't try to speak to her. It was a bumpy flight and there was a warning to passengers to keep their seat belts fastened. Rose gripped hers with both hands and started every time someone buzzed for assistance from the cabin crew. She picked at the food that was offered and left most of it, even when Mrs Luca warned her it would be hours before the next opportunity to eat. The very thought of food made Rose feel nauseous.

In her head, Rose chanted over and over again, *please let me be safe, please let me be safe*, and she shuddered with relief when the announcement was made that they were coming in to land. She suddenly wished she could see out of the window, and wondered if the rabbit was still living near the runway.

There was a hefty bump, a deafening roar of engines and a long, long wait for the plane to come to a halt.

Finally, Mrs Luca leant across the aisle. 'Up you get, Anna,' she said. 'Be sure not to lose us in the rush.'

If only I could, Rose thought. Then, as she stepped out of the plane and on to Romanian soil, she made a silent vow: *This is my home. I will never leave again.*

Chapter 31

For the next three days, Rose and Mrs Luca went back and forth between their hotel and the theatre where they would be performing.

'We need to get used to playing in a different venue,' said Mrs Luca. 'It's one thing playing in the comfort of your own home, but another thing completely to play in a big auditorium. The more we rehearse here, the happier you'll feel.'

Rose was very unhappy when she saw how many seats there were in the theatre, especially as Mrs Luca told her that it was the smallest of the venues they'd booked, and one where she had been particularly well received during the early part of her career.

'We'll start small to build up your confidence, and finish somewhere three times the size,' she said enthusiastically, with a distant look in her eyes.

Rose was appalled at the idea of performing in front of so many people. However much she wanted to follow in Nicu's footsteps, it wasn't supposed to be like this. She was appalled too to see posters outside the theatre, featuring a photograph of Mrs Luca as she was many years ago, seated at the piano, with an inset portrait of herself playing the violin, and another of herself and Mrs Luca together – a photograph from her birthday. She could read enough of the words to know that they said something about *mother and daughter*.

While they rehearsed, members of the theatre staff occasionally stopped work to listen and show their approval. Two older members recalled being present at a previous performance by Mrs Luca, and showered her with compliments, going on to say that her daughter had obviously inherited her talent. When they asked Rose direct questions about herself and she failed to respond, Mrs Luca explained that her daughter was very shy.

Victoria had been incredibly sulky since their arrival, and took every opportunity to have a dig at Rose, who had the misfortune to be sharing a room with her, much to the dismay of both girls. Rose had expected nothing else, but there was nowhere to escape to in the hotel, especially in the evenings after dinner, when Mr and Mrs Luca left them to it while they disappeared downstairs to the bar.

Mrs Luca had begun to talk about reintegrating Rose into the family and letting bygones be bygones.

'If we're to perform together, then we must find a way to live together without all the problems that beset us before. I'm sure you'd prefer to live as one of the family and not as an outcast, Anna. Do you think when we get back home we can start over again?'

Rose nodded. She would have agreed to anything just to be left in peace to work out how she could be reunited with her family and friends. Mrs Luca gave her a big hug and promised she would try her best as well.

'We'll all try our best. Won't we, Victoria?'

Looking past her, Rose saw the girl's face contort.

'I think you might change your mind,' Victoria said coolly.

'What makes you say that, darling?' Mrs Luca wanted to know.

'You'll find out sooner or later, Mother.' Victoria said the word 'Mother' so scornfully, even Mrs Luca looked taken aback.

*

On the morning of the first concert, Mrs Luca and Rose went to the theatre early for a final rehearsal, and to be on hand while lighting and sound checks were carried out. They returned to the hotel at lunchtime to meet up with Mr Luca, who had spent most of his mornings on business matters, and Victoria, who had spent most of hers in bed. Mr Luca was unaccountably cheerful, and announced that he was going to take them all to the best restaurant in town for lunch.

'I've arranged for some very important people to come to our little concert,' he said, 'including a recording company and a bucket-load of journalists. I want to raise a glass to our success.'

'Shouldn't we do that afterwards?' Mrs Luca cautioned.

'Oh, don't be such a wet blanket, Daphne,' scoffed her husband. 'It'll be too late afterwards. The girls will be ready for bed.'

'Not me, Daddy,' Victoria protested. 'I'm not a baby.'

They set out for their lunch, Mr Luca and Victoria in front, arm in arm, Mrs Luca walking with Rose, talking non-stop. Rose realised she must be anxious about their performance later on. It was a beautiful late summer day. The route to the restaurant took them through a small park, where couples were lazing in the sunshine and where families were stretched out on the grass, enjoying picnics. Rose would much rather have joined them than go to an expensive restaurant where she'd be completely out of place, even after months of instruction from Mrs Luca. She cheered herself up by following the antics of a squirrel that was darting acrobatically along the branches of a tree, leaping down to the ground to pick up titbits, then scrambling up the trunk of another tree before repeating the whole process.

'They're such pests, aren't they?' observed Mrs Luca. 'The damage they do to the plants in our garden just doesn't bear thinking about.'

'They're *vermin*, aren't they, Mummy?' Victoria said, turning round and casting a glance at Rose.

On reaching the restaurant, they were shown to a table by the window. Numerous knives, forks, spoons and glasses were laid out in front of them. Rose had no idea what she was supposed to do with them all. A waiter handed her a menu. She opened it, only to find that the list of dishes was too extensive and incomprehensible to her with her limited reading ability. She stared at it, hoping that some of the words would begin to make sense.

'What are you going to have, Anna?' Victoria asked, her lip curling.

Rose shrugged as though undecided.

'Well, I'm going to have my favourite,' said Mrs Luca.

'How very unadventurous,' Mr Luca responded.

'There's no point in choosing something different and being disappointed,' Mrs Luca replied. 'I shall have the vegetable soup to start with, followed by fish cakes, and then I shall give the performance of a lifetime!'

'Well, I'll have the breaded chicken and I'm going to start with dumpling soup,' said Victoria.

The waiter was hovering by the table, ready to take their orders. When it came to Rose's turn, she pointed at two random dishes on the menu, and hadn't a clue what food would be put before her. Mrs Luca gazed at her in surprise.

'What's Anna having, Mummy?' Victoria asked.

'Lambs' kidneys on toast to start with, followed by veal liver as a main,' Mrs Luca replied. 'Are you sure, Anna?'

Rose nodded her head confidently, though she already knew she'd made a big mistake.

Victoria snorted. 'What an offally good choice!'

'Good joke, darling,' praised Mr Luca, who had plumped for a selection of cold meats to start with and the pork tenderloin. He picked up his glass, which the waiter had filled with champagne, and raised a toast: 'Here's to a successful evening, a successful tour and a growing bank balance.'

'Here's to a happy family.' Mrs Luca beamed.

Rose raised her water glass and clinked it against her guardians' glasses.

'We'll never be a happy family,' said Victoria quietly, without raising her glass.

'Not now, darling,' her father warned.

'Why not now?' she asked.

'It's not the time or the place,' Mr Luca said firmly.

'It's never the time or the place. You never allow me to say what I think or feel.'

'I think you get plenty of opportunities,' said Mrs Luca.

'I'm not talking about you not being my mother,' Victoria persisted.

'Quiet!' Mr Luca ordered.

Victoria put her hand in her pocket, took it back out and placed her closed fist down on the table.

'Is this some sort of a game?' Mrs Luca asked.

'But we don't play games,' said Victoria. 'Or do we?'

She opened her fist. In it lay Mrs Luca's gold brooch.

'What's going on?' demanded Mr Luca. 'Where did that come from?'

Victoria stared hard at Rose. Mr and Mrs Luca followed her stare. Rose wanted to be sick.

'I brought it with me,' Victoria announced triumphantly. 'And this.' From her bag she produced the silver jug.

'What on earth are you talking about?' snapped Mr Luca.

'I was going to plant them among Anna's clothes, but I've got rather bored with that game, so I thought I'd surprise you all by bringing them to the table.' Victoria grinned at her parents while they took in what she had said.

'You mean –'

'Are you trying to tell us that you're the thief?' Mr Luca blustered.

'I wasn't really thieving, Daddy.' Victoria pouted. 'I just moved them around a bit. My bracelet too, but I seem to have lost track of that.' She stared at Rose again.

'But why?'

'Why do you think? Because I'm fed up with not mattering. I'm fed up with Daphne and her projects. I'm fed up with being asked to share my life with any waifs and strays who drop into your lives. You married my mother and you were happy, but she got ill and died. I know it wasn't your fault she died, and you were

208

devastated too. But then you married again. The trouble is, I've never been enough for Daphne and you're always too busy with your work.'

'That's not fair,' protested Mrs Luca. 'I've always tried my best to make you feel loved.'

'But you haven't *loved* me,' said Victoria. 'You haven't loved me because your love died with Anna, and it's stayed locked up in that shrine of yours for years.'

It took Rose a moment or two to realise what was being said, and then she understood that she shared not only her new birthday with Mrs Luca's daughter, but also her new name.

'*I* love you, darling,' said Mr Luca hotly.

'I know you do, Daddy, in your way, but work and business are always more important. And now this silly tour is more important. There's always something more important.'

Just then the waiter arrived with their food. When he put Rose's plate in front of her, she had a desperate urge to hurl it across the table at Victoria. All the pain the girl had caused her, all the terrible accusations she had made! Rose didn't feel sorry for her, not for one second. She didn't feel sorry for any of them. They deserved each other. They were destroying each other with a thousand cuts, and not one of them knew how to stop it.

'I don't understand why you didn't just talk to us about how you felt, instead of trying to blame poor Anna for something she didn't do,' said Mrs Luca.

'Poor Anna? Lucky Anna! She's plucked from some miserable Gypsy existence to be pampered rotten, and you call her poor!'

'But you made us think she was a thief!' Mrs Luca tried to put her hand on Rose's arm, but she pulled away. 'What about the doll's house? Was that you too?' She hardly dared ask the question.

Victoria nodded. 'All that time it took to put it together, yet it was so easy to knock it all down.'

'Never mind the doll's house, what about the fish?' Mr Luca demanded.

'That wasn't me!' Victoria flared. 'I wouldn't do that. That probably was Anna. I've seen her sticking her fingers in the water.'

Rose didn't bother to deny it. *Let them think what they like. At least they've been proved wrong over the missing items.* She was tired of listening to them.

'It was probably your precious Goran,' Mr Luca growled, turning on his wife. 'I'll probably find they're *all* dead by the time we get home. Well, a fine celebration this turned out to be.'

None of them knew what to say any more. Their food sat in front of them, untouched, until Victoria began to tuck in.

Mrs Luca pushed hers away.

'I can't eat,' she muttered. She took her brooch from the table and Rose looked on as she very deliberately put it in her handbag.

'I told you it doesn't bring you any luck,' said her husband. 'Let's hope it brings better luck this evening.'

Chapter 32

After everything that had happened, Rose was amazed they were going ahead with the concert. Mr Luca insisted, saying it would be wrong to let the public down and that too many other things were contingent upon its success. Mrs Luca scarcely spoke. Victoria was quiet too, though from the tilt of her chin Rose was convinced she felt no remorse over what she had done.

'Don't expect me to say sorry to you,' she told Rose. 'Because I won't. Ever.'

They passed the remainder of the afternoon resting in their hotel. When the time came to leave for the theatre, Rose wondered how she'd be able to string two notes together, and was sure Mrs Luca would struggle to move her fingers across the piano keys. Poor Mrs Luca. Rose doubted she would ever get it right where Victoria – or her husband – were concerned. She tried to free her mind of the events of the day as they walked along the street. She wanted to focus on how she might escape from this family that had ensnared her and heaped its torments upon her.

Rose hadn't found an answer by the time they reached the theatre door. She was beginning to doubt there was an answer. People blustered around them from the moment they entered the auditorium and nerves began to interfere with her thoughts. Was she really going to step out on to the stage and play in front of all the people who would soon be filling the seats? She thought about Nicu and Esme and how they had embraced every performance, but they were adults and had practised for years. She looked at the clock at the rear of the theatre, its hands ticking inexorably onward, and wished she could climb up and turn them back.

She was ushered to her dressing room, where a woman, under Mrs Luca's instructions, helped her to change into a severe black dress and tied back her hair. Nadia, as she was called, chattered continuously while she applied some colour to Rose's cheeks and lips.

'The lights will drain all your natural colour even though you're quite dark,' she explained. 'We don't want you looking like a ghost, do we? You're very brave at your age to go out and play to all those people. I'd

213

be scared! My knees would be knocking together so hard they'd be black and blue. Your mum looks even more terrified than you do, poor thing. I hear she used to be very good when she was younger. I expect she wants to show she still has it in her. I played the violin once. My dad said it sounded like a cat having its tail run over. He was right too. We can't all be talented, though, can we? Not in the same way, at least. That's your bell going. Means you've got five minutes. Good luck then, my lovely. Hope it goes well for you.'

Mrs Luca collected Rose from the dressing room, saying breathlessly, 'I know you're not joining me until halfway through, but you can listen from the wings.'

Nadia's right, Rose thought. *She is shaking.*

Mrs Luca took Rose's hand and whispered, 'Good luck.'

Rose squeezed her hand back and watched as she took to the stage amid rapturous applause.

Mrs Luca was good – very good – but cold. Rose sat in the wings and tried to feel the music she was hearing. However, there was no passion in Mrs Luca's performance, no individual voice telling the world, 'This is me. I'm baring my soul to you. I demand that you listen.'

Has her music always been that way? Rose wondered. *Have all the bad things that have happened in her life made it impossible for her to express herself? Was she happy and free once, and did her music reflect that? Was that why she had been so praised in the past?*

All too soon it was Rose's turn to join her. Rose was petrified. Mr Luca pushed her in the back, and she found herself stranded on the stage like a startled rabbit. A glare of lights blinded her at first, then, as her eyes grew accustomed to them, she noticed a shadowland of heads all turned towards her, watching and waiting.

'Come forward,' Mrs Luca hissed at her.

Rose edged her way towards the piano. As she did, Mrs Luca stood up and turned to the audience.

'I want to introduce you to my daughter, Anna, who I'm proud to say has inherited my musical talent and is making her debut this evening.' Mrs Luca paused. 'As you will have heard, Anna is unable to speak. She has never been able to speak. She was born mute, poor child. But she lets her music speak for her. I hope you'll love what she has to say . . .'

Mrs Luca sat down again at the piano.

Rose couldn't move. She was stunned by what she had just heard.

'Ready?' Mrs Luca whispered.

Rose grimaced. She was there on stage for all to see and had no option but to go through with it. She offered a slight curtsy to the audience as she had been told to do, while they clapped encouragingly.

Mrs Luca played the opening bar of a piece they had practised over and over again. Rose closed her eyes and tried to picture herself in a big open field, playing for no one except the birds in the air. She held the bow in place, took a deep breath and, when her moment came, she began.

The first few bars were shaky, Rose knew, and she battled to keep the bow from quivering. She could feel the tension in the audience as they willed her to get it right and exceed their expectations. She fought to hold herself together, to allow the music to take over. At last, she gained control and was able to move the bow without it juddering against the strings.

Mrs Luca hit a wrong note and glared at her, but Rose knew she wasn't at fault. And then, as she caught sight of Mr Luca, now sitting in the front row of the audience with Victoria, a picture of Nicu filled her head. Nicu playing the violin; Nicu whipping the crowd into a frenzy, then stroking them into tranquillity; Nicu weaving spells with his music and making the world a happy place.

There was a break in the music between the first and second movements. Before Mrs Luca could lay her fingers back down on the piano keys, Rose took a step forward on the stage, stamped her feet, shook her head so that her hair fell loose, then struck her bow violently downward against the strings of her violin.

This is for you, Papa.

She began to play, not the music Mr and Mrs Luca had demanded, but the music of her father, of her family, of her people. Somewhere behind her, Mrs Luca told her to stop, but in that moment she had no power over her. Rose was like a sorcerer with a magic wand. Nothing could touch her any more. She was doing what Nicu wanted and he would have been proud of her, just as she was of him the day before two monsters of people destroyed her family.

She played the final heartbreaking note, and slowly lowered the violin.

There was silence.

At last, someone clapped, then someone else cheered.

The whole audience followed, rising to their feet as though linked by some magical cord. Rose caught Mrs Luca's eye. The woman whose project she had been looked utterly defeated. In front of Rose, Mr Luca and Victoria were the only people still sitting.

Gradually, the ovation came to an end and nobody knew what to do. Except for Rose. Somewhere deep inside her, something was struggling to get out. She opened her mouth and whispered something which nobody could hear.

She tried again, louder this time, fighting to control her breathing and find her voice. 'My name is Rose.'

Then louder still, and bold. 'My name is Rose. Not Anna. I want to go home to my people. These are not my people. Please let me go home.'

She watched as Mrs Luca fled from the stage, and said again, 'My name is Rose.'

Read on for an extract from the brilliant

Spilled Water

by Sally Grindley . . .

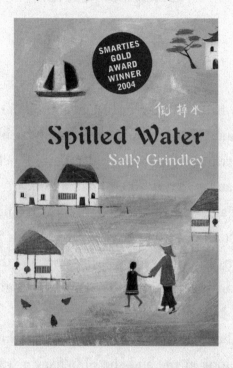

'Deserving Smarties Gold Award winner.
A powerful story'
The Times

OUT NOW

Chapter One
To Market

I loved my baby brother, until Uncle took me to market and sold me. He was the bright, shiny pebble in the water, the twinkling star in the sky. Until Uncle took me to market and sold me. Then I hated him.

'Lu Si-yan,' Uncle greeted me early one summer morning, 'today is a big day for you. From today, you must learn to find your own way in the muddy whirlpool of life. Your mother and I have given you a good start. Now it is your turn.'

My mother stood in the shadows of our kitchen, but she didn't look at me and she didn't say a word. Uncle took me tightly by the wrist. As he led me from the house, my mother reached out her hand towards me and clawed the air as though trying to pull me back. Then she picked up my little brother and hid behind the door, but I saw her face wither with pain and, in that moment, fear gripped my heart.

'Where are you taking me, Uncle Ba?' I cried.

'It's for the best,' he replied, his mouth set grimly.

'You're hurting my arm,' I cried.

He pulled me past the scorched patchwork terraces of my family's smallholding, scattering hens and ducks along the way, and out on to the dusty track that led steeply up to the road. There, we walked, Uncle brisk and businesslike, me dragging my feet in protest, until we came to the bus-stop.

'Where are we going, Uncle Ba?' I whimpered this time.

'To market,' he said.

'What are we going to buy?' I asked.

Chapter Two

The Happiest Soul
on Earth

Everybody loved my father. My mother used to say that he was the happiest soul on earth. When you were with him he made you feel happy too.

When there was just me, he used to lift me on to his shoulders and gallop down to the river, where he picked me up by the armpits and dangled my feet in the water. I screamed at the cold, but then he put my feet in his jacket pockets, one in each side, and we galloped off again, laughing all the way.

When there was just me, he sat me in his rickshaw and cycled along the road, weaving from one side to the other, bump, bump, bump across the cobbles, singing at the top of his voice. I lurched up and down on the seat, yelling at him to stop but wanting him to carry on.

When there was just me, he taught me to play chess and wei-qi, and sometimes I won, but I knew that he was letting me. We played mahjong with Uncle and my mother. Father and I made silly bird noises every time it came to the 'twittering of the sparrows', while Uncle tutted and my mother rolled her eyes heavenwards in mock exasperation.

We never had much money, but I didn't really notice because neither did anyone else in our village. Father's favourite saying was, 'If you realise that you have enough, you are truly rich', and he believed it. 'We have fresh food and warm clothes, a roof over our heads (a bit leaky when it rains) and a wooden bed to sleep on. What more can we ask for?' he demanded. 'And not only that,' he continued, 'but I have the finest little dumpling of a daughter in the whole of China.'

My parents worked hard to make sure that we always had enough. Father set off early in the morning, his farming tools over his shoulder, to tend the dozens of tiny terraces of vegetables that straggled higgledy-piggledy over the hillside above and below our house. He dug and sowed and weeded and cropped throughout the numbing cold of winter and the suffocating heat of summer. In the middle of the day, he returned home clutching triumphantly a gigantic sheaf of pakchoi, a basin of bright green beans, or a bucket full of melon-sized turnips.

'Your father can grow the biggest, tastiest vegetables on a piece of land the size of a silk handkerchief,' Mother used to say, and I would skip off to help him because I wanted one day to grow the biggest, tastiest vegetables as well.

Mostly, I spent the mornings with Mother, feeding the hens and ducks and collecting their eggs which were scattered around our yard. There were slops to be taken out to our pig and fresh straw to be laid. Once a week, along with our neighbours and their children, we carried our clothes down to the river to wash them. That was the best day. When it was hot, we children pulled off the clothes we were wearing and charged into the river, splashing wildly and shrieking our heads off. We learnt to swim very young and raced backwards and forwards through the sparkling waters. As soon as we were back on the shore, our mothers attacked us with soap, then we dashed into the water again to rinse it off, before running around in the sun to dry. In winter, the river sometimes froze for days on end. Some of the older children went skating on it, but Father said they were foolish because they might fall in.

Mother was ready with soup and rice when my father returned at midday. He used to sit me on his knee and ask me what I had been up to all morning. I made up stories about fighting dragons and escaping from haunted temples and he would sit there saying, 'Did you? Did you really? What a morning that must have been!' until we dissolved into fits of giggles and Father said, 'I hope the rest of the day will be quieter for you.'

In the afternoons, Father returned to his terraces, or he would walk several miles with other villagers to work on the rice fields that they shared. Mother went to the village to shop and to gossip, and I went with her to play with my friends. Nobody minded us dashing in and out of the shops in a boisterous game of hide-and-seek, and the old men smiled as we peered over their shoulders to watch them playing cards on wobbly foldaway tables in the street.

Back home again, Mother and I prepared the evening meal, ready for my father's return. Sometimes, if he was early enough, he took his boat out on the river to fish.

He would let me go with him if I promised to be ever so quiet. Once we caught the biggest carp anyone in the village had ever seen. If we stood it on its tail it was taller than me! We took it to market and sold it for so much money that Father was able to buy us each a new pair of shoes.

Father never worked on Sunday afternoons. If necessary, he worked still harder during the week in order to free himself for his 'family time'. On Sundays, he sharpened all our kitchen knives, selected the very best vegetables from our farm, killed one of our chickens, and set to work with spices and herbs and ginger and garlic in preparation for our evening meal. This was his favourite time. We would sit at the table and talk to him as he chopped away. We were not allowed to help.

'You have had to prepare my meals all week,' he would say to my mother. 'Now it is my turn to prepare your meal.'

If ever Mother argued that he had been working all week long on the farm and should put his feet up, he simply said, 'That is different, and in any case I enjoy cooking. I want to cook, and I want you to put your feet up.'

Mother grumbled good-humouredly at his stubbornness, but we knew that he loved every minute of his weekly role as chef. And he was good at it. The meals we ate on Sunday evenings were the best, Mother was happy to admit it. When they were over, we sat down as a family and watched television. It didn't matter what was on – it was just the being there together that we loved.

Chapter Three
To Market

Uncle remained silent, sucking hard on a cigarette, leaving my question hanging in the heavy morning air, until a bus came along and he pushed me aboard. Two women I recognised from a nearby village were already sitting inside. They immediately asked us where we were going. Uncle said a name that meant nothing to me, while making it clear that he did not wish to discuss his business any further. I heard one of the women whisper that, my goodness, we were going on a long journey, and the two of them wondered aloud what on earth we might be going all that way for. Uncle ignored them, while I tried to make sense of the disturbing turn of events that had thrown my life into confusion.

I gazed out of the window, slightly comforted to realise that the landscape was still familiar. Father and I had come this far many a time in the past, bump, bump, bump in his rickshaw. Then the bus stopped and the two women clambered off, waving goodbye to me, wishing me a pleasant journey. They headed in the direction of a street lined with colourful stalls. I saw that it was the market where my father always used to sell his vegetables and where we had sold his enormous carp.

'Why aren't we going to that market?' I asked.

'Too small,' said Uncle brusquely.

The bus rumbled on again, leaving the world I knew behind it, to climb, twist, speed through countryside, villages and towns I had never seen before. Gradually the motion of the bus sent me to sleep.

I woke up to find myself stretched out across Uncle's lap, his arm curled round my shoulder. When he saw that I was awake, he pulled his arm away abruptly, as though he didn't want me to think that he was showing any affection for me. I sat up and looked around. The bus was empty apart from us. Outside, it was growing dark. How many hours had we been travelling? We'd left home soon after breakfast. We'd had nothing to eat since. I was ravenous.

'How much further?' I said. 'I'm starving.'

'Not long,' said Uncle. He reached in his pocket and gave me a piece of cake which my mother must have baked.

'When are we going home again?' I asked.

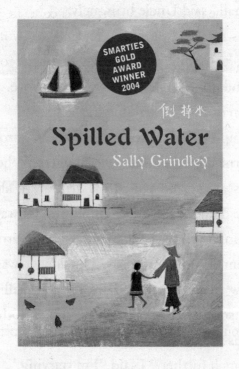

OUT NOW

Q & A with
Sally Grindley

Where did the inspiration for this book come from?

I watched a film called *Gypsy Caravan: When the Road Bends*, which follows five Gypsy bands on tour in North America, where they astound audiences with their music. The film celebrates the best in Gypsy culture and the diversity of the Romani people. I wanted to write about their music and explore what a loss it would be to someone who grew up with it if it were suddenly taken away from them.

Are your characters ever based on real people?

No, but characteristics of people I know are undoubtedly woven into my fictional characters.

Why do you write about children in different settings around the world?

I'm inspired by the resilience of children wherever they come from, but children from very poor countries have to deal with the most dreadful traumas and horrendous living conditions, often from a very young age. I think it's important that, as world citizens, children who are more fortunate should have an understanding of the sheer everyday struggle to survive that other children experience.

When did you start writing?

I've always enjoyed writing – essays at school, poetry in my teens, children's plays at university. I didn't make a conscious decision to become an author. I worked for a children's book club for 17 years and had an idea for a children's book while I was driving one day. It all took off from there . . .

Is there a particular routine involved in your writing process (e.g. a favourite pen, lucky charm or special jumper)?

None whatsoever, though I find it easier to write in the same place – currently my dining room table. I try to be disciplined with my writing.

If someone wants to be a writer, what would be your number-one tip for them?

It's like any other thing you want to be good at – sport, music, cooking – you have to practise, practise, practise, and you have to read, read, read. Read anything and everything!